SECOND CHANCE

SECOND CHANCE

Marc Terry Sr.

SECOND CHANCE

iUniverse books may be ordered through booksellers or by contacting:

iUniverse
1663 Liberty Drive
Bloomington, IN 47403
www.iuniverse.com
844-349-9409

*Because of the dynamic nature of the Internet, any web addresses or
links contained in this book may have changed since publication and
may no longer be valid. The views expressed in this work are solely those
of the author and do not necessarily reflect the views of the publisher,
and the publisher hereby disclaims any responsibility for them.*

*Any people depicted in stock imagery provided by Getty Images are
models, and such images are being used for illustrative purposes only.
Certain stock imagery © Getty Images.*

ISBN: 978-1-6632-1256-6 (sc)
ISBN: 978-1-6632-1257-3 (e)

Library of Congress Control Number: 2020923672

Print information available on the last page.

iUniverse rev. date: 12/01/2020

Kevin thought to himself, *I should at least call my sisters and tell them 'Hi'. Let them know I love them.*

He knew full well in his heart that it would be his way of saying his goodbyes as his eyes fixated on the half-full hypodermic needle in his hand.

Just as well, he thought, *no more of them worrying where I am or how I'm doing, if I'm in jail or even still alive, for that matter. This*, as he glanced at the needle, *would bring them peace*, he thought, as he tried to summon the courage to go through with his plan.

I should do this Friday, he thought, *that would give me time to settle some things. At least I'll get to celebrate my birthday tomorrow. WHAT THINGS?!,* he laughed at the idea. *Isn't that just like you, even now, procrastinating. No. No calls. No long goodbyes. Just get it done!*

He pulled the belt tight to his upper arm, as he had seen people do in the movies, and poised the needle over the largest vein he could see. He surveyed the room. It was dark and damp, the smell of unwashed, musty laundry, and the ever-present smell of what could only be dead rodents, permeated the still air. The spot served him well during the harsh winter, though.

He calls this his *abandominium*. It's just one of the many boarded up row houses left to decay in Baltimore's inner city. "How in the hell did you end up here in got-damned Baltimore?!" he said aloud and laughed.

His face went from that smile that made everyone around him smile in his younger days, to a grim expression as he faced the task at hand. Suicide by self-administered lethal injection. His drug of choice was heroin. *May as well go out nodding,* he thought. *Painless. I'm here, then I'm gone. Nothing to it.* He returned his attention to his arm, being careful to place the needle right at the vein. He hated needles, always did. *Need to pay attention,* he thought; *I don't want to have to stick myself twice.*

"I'll tell you how you wound up in Baltimore!" a voice bellowed from downstairs.

"Who the hell is that?!" yelled Kevin. He heard footsteps pass the foyer and begin to ascend the stairs.

"It's me!" the voice said as it laughed.

"ME is 'bout to get dead if ME come up here!" Kevin yelled back at the approaching voice as he scrambled to his feet and grabbed his knife from under his makeshift bed.

"Still got that temper of yours, huh man? How's that worked out for you?" the voice bellowed.

Kevin hid the needle atop the door trim at the room's entrance as he stood in the threshold waiting for the stranger to reach the top of the stairs.

"You the police or something?" Kevin asked as the man's hat came into view at the top of the stairs.

"Nah, not the police" as he came into full view at the landing.

Blue hat, gray suit, white shirt, blue tie, gray shoes. Indistinguishable facial features. About 6'3" to 6'5" and around 245 pounds. Lean. *I can take him*, Kevin thought to himself. He remembered what his father told him as a child, *'No one can beat you fighting until they beat you fighting'* which was his father's way of saying fear no one.

Kevin felt a little more at ease, as he could see that this man wasn't someone of authority.

"The hell you want, slim?" Kevin said as he cuffed the knife behind his right arm to hide it.

"What you gonna stab me Kevin? Cut me? Come on man..." the stranger said with his hands out smiling.

Kevin looked at the stranger for a minute and for some unknown reason, he trusted that he wasn't there to harm him, which struck him as odd because he'd learned in his life to never trust anyone. He turned his back to the stranger and walked back into the room, placed the knife back under the rumpled sheets and stepped to the middle of the room.

"What you want man?" Kevin asked.

The stranger removed his hat. "May I come in?" he asked.

Kevin turned from him and said, "Oh, you've got manners now, huh? I don't remember hearing a knock at the front door. The hell you want?!" Kevin said.

The stranger stepped into the room. As Kevin sat to face him on the edge of the bed, he motioned the man to have a seat. The man surveyed the condition of the room, smiled and said, "If it's quite alright, I'll stand."

Kevin was suddenly cognizant of the appearance of his living quarters and said, "These ain't the five-star accommodations you're used to, huh man?"

The stranger laughed a little. "Oh, I've seen worse, not by much, I'll give you that, but worse."

Kevin laughed a little and said, "Well…."

"Bridges, my name is Bridges," the stranger interrupted.

"Ok, Mr. Bridges, to what do I owe your visit? Hope you're not here to rob me of all these riches you see laid out before you."

The stranger smiled. "Bridges, just plain Bridges, and funny thing is I am here to, in a way, collect on something you owe."

Kevin's face went flush. He glanced over at the place he had returned the knife and looked back at Bridges, who was now standing within 4 feet of him.

"If you'd feel more comfortable with that knife in your hand, you can retrieve it", Bridges said as he stepped away from Kevin.

Kevin stood up, never taking his eyes from Bridges, got his knife, sat back down, and slipped it under his right thigh with the handle sticking out. "You never know, I might", Kevin said.

"Fine. Now that you're more comfortable and at ease, I need to talk to you about a few things. About what you owe me", Bridges said as he took his place in the room again.

"This is probably going to take a while and I've travelled a long way." He said as he looked at the lone chair in the room that seemed to double as Kevin's dirty laundry basket.

"Stay calm…" He said in a reassuring voice as the clothes flew off the chair and into the corner.

"WHAT THE HELL?!" Kevin said as he jumped to his feet with the knife in his hand. "WHO ARE YOU, THE DEVIL!!?" Kevin said with his eyes wide open.

Bridges turned his back to Kevin, pulled a handkerchief from his pocket, and wiped the seat of the chair. He went to return the square to his pocket, then looked at it in disgust and tossed it in the corner with the other clothes. He sat, pulled a cigarette from his jacket pocket, took a drag, and exhaled a large cloud of smoke.

"Can't kick this habit for nothing. I know you know the struggle. Have one?", Bridges asked as he extended the pack toward Kevin.

Kevin sat back down with a look of shock on his face. Bridges shrugged and returned the pack to his pocket.

"So, you're the Devil, huh? …Lighting cigarettes out of thin air, moving stuff around…. All that Twilight Zone shit, huh man?" Kevin said.

"I said stay calm, didn't I?! No. I'm not the Devil, the Vice Devil, a Demon, or any other representative of Hell or the Occult. I am Bridges and my job is to fine-tune things. Make corrections of the sort."

Kevin looked at him with puzzlement. "Corrections??"

Bridges offered the cigarettes again. "You sure?"

"Nah, man, I'll pass. Some weed could help me deal with your crazy shit, though!" Kevin said.

"You don't smoke weed. And you don't do Heroin, either." Bridges said as he extended his open hand and showed Kevin the syringe. "So, you were going to take your life tonight, huh?"

Kevin slumped a little. "Yup...yeah I was. Still am matter of fact. I'm sick of this crap. Not doing another winter like this, that's for damn sure. I'm done."

Bridges nodded his head up and down as he crushed the cigarette under his foot. "You thought about your sisters? Or Mrs. Vance, who you get groceries and pick up prescriptions for? And what about little Chris? You're the only male role model he's got. What about all these people Kevin? You think about them?"

Kevin looked down at the floor, it blurred, and he watched as the first teardrop fell before he quickly wiped his eyes.

"They're all better off without me. Every single one of them. What the hell makes you think I hadn't thought about that?!" Kevin asked angrily.

Bridges looked out the window. He pulled out a cigarette and handed it to Kevin, who, out of habit, reached for his lighter before noticing it was already lit. Kevin inhaled deeply, then leaned back on the pile of clean clothes on the bed. "Man, look, I STILL don't know who the hell you are, and why the hell you're here questioning me and doing all these *magic* tricks and shit!! What the hell you want, man?!"

Bridges walked to the window and looked down into the street. "We need to address some things before we go any further. Kevin, your mother was a great woman. She was your heart. The compassion and empathy you have is a direct result of her nurturing ways. Your father was a strong, hard-working, good man. His strength is what empowered you to endure all that you've been through and push forward. The two of them combined instilled in you two tigers. The problem is, when you get hurt, you act out in aggression. That's never worked out well for you. Two, you've always put too much pressure on people. You expect too much of them. You look for other people to act and react to situations the way you would. Then you get disappointed when they seldom do. You need to learn to accept people as they are. Don't burden them with who you want them to be. I know you've heard the saying,' *when someone shows you who they are, accept it,*' haven't you? Don't try to change people, man. You understand?"

Kevin took another drag from his cigarette, looked at Bridges, and grinned. "You're talking to me like I'm going to need all this advice in the future. As you can clearly see…" Kevin glanced at the syringe in Bridges hand, "I don't really have any plans for the future. You feel me?"

Bridges turned back to Kevin and smiled. "Well…just try to keep what I said in mind and apply it ok?"

Kevin looked at him and sat up groggily. "Dude, you may as well be telling that dead rat that's in here somewhere to watch what he eats from now on! I'm ghost, Champ! Checking out of Hotel Shithouse tonight! Believe that. Like you said, 'when people tell you, blah, blah, blah…believe them! BELIEVE ME, man! We done here? I'm a busy got damn man, and I got things to do, you understand?" Kevin said with a stupid smirk on his face.

"And dude, I'm not even going to ask you how you know about all my people. You rap too got damn much. Don't feel like hearing it. Like I said, I'm busy."

Chain-smoking bama, Kevin said under his breath.

Bridges blew the smoke out, laughing. "Bama, damn right I chain smoke!"

Kevin looked up in surprise. "Oh, ok, so you're a DC dude, huh?"

Bridges smiled. "Would you believe me if I said I've been around before DC was DC? I pick up stuff along the way. Like 'Bama'; I like that. Describes a lot of you dudes."

Kevin sat up straight. "Ain't no Bama here man! I'm from Uptown!"

Bridges gave Kevin a blank stare. "Seriously? You're going to tell ME where you're from man? Let's see, you went to Takoma Elementary; your best friend was Rick. After that to Rabaut

Jr High, which you didn't like, so you went to Paul. Realized you made a mistake; too late. Went to Coolidge High. Joined the Navy. Got Married. Got Divorced. Messed around and got re-married. Got divorced again. Then you took a downward spiral and landed in beautiful downtown Baltimore in these lovely accommodations. I left a lot of stuff out; want me to fill in the blanks?"

Kevin stared at Bridges with his eyes wide open, then his face went blank. "Yeah, actually, you left out that my brother is gone, my mother and father are gone, and I have a daughter and son that don't want anything to do with me! How about those facts for life highlights?! You know what?! To hell with all this! Dude, I'm 48 got damn years old! Tell me again why the hell you are here messing with me?!"

Bridges took his time walking to and taking his seat. He scooted the chair so that he could be within 2 feet of Kevin. Face-to-face. He put his head down, spun his hat in his hand, looked back into Kevin's eyes and said, "Look man, a while ago you were supposed to do something. Something that would make something else happen in the future, or past as it is. You didn't do it. We tried to go another route to make this event happen, but it failed. YOU have to do it. There's no other way. So here I am."

Kevin plucked his cigarette butt across the room. "Something in the past?? What the hell you talking about, exactly?! Spell it out!! What the hell was I supposed to do in the past that's so got damn important? And how and WHY am I supposed to do something about that now?" You know what? You're right; you aren't the Devil. You're the got damn Riddler! What the hell, man?!"

Bridges spun his hat in his hand again. "I can't tell you exactly what you were supposed to do. It just doesn't work that way. And this…me having this conversation with you about it, this doesn't happen often. See, YOU messed up. And I've got to fine tune stuff so that things go along as planned."

Kevin looked at him side-eyed. "Ok magic man, so what's next? You should know that as soon as you leave…"

Bridges' expression got serious. "Listen to me closely. Remember what I said, don't make yourself obvious, don't tip your hand. You got that!

Goodbye Kevin."

Bridges stood and extended his hand for a shake.

"Bout time…" Kevin said as he stood to shake Bridges hand. They shook.

"You have a busy day tomorrow, Kevin Allen. Stay calm." Bridges' hand turned to light, grew bright, then dimmed. Kevin passed out at the sight.

Kevin awakened slowly. He looked over to see the ceiling light hanging just a few feet above him in the center of the room. Everything seemed familiar–the smells, the covers, the mattress. Kevin rolled to the edge of the bed and looked down at the floor. *That was one WILD dream!* he thought to himself.

"What the…?" he whispered as he looked around the room, noticing Graham Central Station painted on the wall, a pair of

Ked's deck tennis shoes beside the bed, and polo cologne on the dresser. "What the hell?!" He said louder.

"What, man?", Kevin heard in a groggy voice below him.

His heart raced. That sounded like David's voice. *No way; I must be still dreaming. That couldn't be...* "David?", Kevin said softly.

"5 more minutes, man." He heard come from the bed below him.

"DAVID!!!" Kevin threw his covers off and leaped from the top bunk and jumped on his brother hugging him. "David, man..." He said, crying uncontrollably.

"Hey man, get the...get the hell off me! GET...OFF...ME!!! MAAAA!!!" David yelled at the top of his voice as he tried to wrestle his brother off him.

"You two had better cut all that noise out and get ready for school!" Kevin heard his mother yell from downstairs.

"MA!!!" Kevin jumped from David and raced down the steps to catch his mother in the hallway putting on her jacket preparing to go to work. He grabbed her and almost knocked her off her feet. "MA!!!!!!" He hugged her tightly and kissed her cheek and her forehead and her hands repeatedly.

"Boy, what's WRONG with...you better get upstairs and put some clothes on yourself! Coming down here in your underwear; I told you about that!", she said trying to look serious, but smiling a little at the unexpected, surprise show of affection.

"Ok...ok...wait...wait...don't go...I'll be right back!", Kevin said as he released her and bounded up the stairs.

"I'm late, Kevin. I've got to drop Jean off and get to work. You all's lunch money is on the table. I'll see you later."

Kevin was upstairs trying desperately to put his pants leg on. He heard the door close and ran to open the bathroom window. He yelled down to his mother smiling excitedly. "I LOVE YOU, MOM!!!"

Kevin's mother looked up with a worried look on her face. "I love you too, Kevin. Hurry up and get ready, ok. And get your brother out of that bed!"

"OK!", Kevin yelled back down as he closed the window.

"What's gotten into him?", Kevin's mom said to his little sister Jean.

"I told you he's crazy", Jean replied.

Kevin's Mom smiled. "Hush up, Jean."

Jean looked at her Mom smiling. "Ok, but he is."

They laughed as they got into the car and left. Kevin turned around to see David with a serious look on his face and in a defensive stance with pants on in the next room. David was 11 months and 4 days younger than Kevin, and about 5 inches shorter. Kevin was tall and skinny. David was built stocky.

"Man, I don't know what the hell is wrong with your ass, but you come in here with that gump shit again and I'm knocking you the hell out!", David warned Kevin.

"David!", Kevin yelled as he ran into the room toward his brother.

David hit Kevin in the lip, knocking him to the floor. Kevin rose up slowly on his hands and wiped his lip. He looked at the blood and smiled up at David. "My man D…"

They got dressed, and David grabbed his lunch money and started for the door.

"You aren't going to hold up for me?", Kevin asked.

"You going to school today? On a Friday?", David asked.

"Yup. Yeah…I guess I am", Kevin responded, realizing that he must still be in high school. *Oh, shit! What year is this? Who's my first period teacher? My can!* Thoughts raced through his mind as he ran back up the stairs to his room. His can, a metal cookie can, is where he kept all his 'important' stuff. *Here it is!* He'd found his class schedule. *What year though?* He thought for a second, then went downstairs and looked on the Fuji bench for the mail. 1978. "It's Friday, 1978", he said aloud. *I'm 16. That puts me in the 11th grade at Coolidge High School. What month though?* He went to the kitchen and found the bag where his Mom kept all the coupons from the Sunday paper. *October. Last Sunday was the 11th, so today is the 16th. October 16th, 1978.* "Bridges! I won't mess up this time!", he said aloud.

"Come on man!", David yelled from the porch.

"I'm coming!", said Kevin.

They talked the whole mile walk to school. Something they almost never did, because David had his interests and friends, and Kevin had his, which were hooking school, trying to get some booty, and having fun. David did the last two in moderation and seemed to be more successful at number two than his brother, despite Kevin's best efforts. David had that nice, country boy 'we can just be cool' approach. Kevin had earned a reputation for trying a little too hard to get sex. His desperation made it a bit rough to come by.

As they walked through the front door of the school, David grabbed Kevin's arm and said, "Hey man, if you ever try to jump on me again like that, I'ma beat your ass for real. Don't do that shit again", he said with a serious look on his face.

"Man, Jean hits harder than you! Get the hell off me!", Kevin said, laughing as he snatched his arm from David and entered the school.

David stood there for a second, shook his head and said aloud, "Man, what the hell…"

Kevin pulled out his schedule.

Homeroom: Mr. Scott

As he walked through the door, Mr. Scott did a double take. "Mr. Allen! To what do we owe the pleasure of your attendance this morning?"

Mr. Scott was one of those teachers that had been in the teaching game too long. Lazy. Didn't care. Just there to collect a paycheck and retire.

"School Board sent me to keep an eye on you." Kevin said as he walked by.

"Watch your mouth young man and take a seat", the teacher said with an annoyed tone.

Kevin thought to himself, *His punk ass talking about 'watch your mouth!' Get the hell outta here, man...damn. Yeah. I gotta watch my mouth. Gotta remember, I'm 16, not 48 anymore. Shit!*

"Sorry, Mr. Allen", Kevin said as he settled in. *You still a wimp, though!* he thought to himself smiling.

"Sorry, Mr. Allen", Kevin heard a female say, mocking him from the next desk. The voice belonged to his buddy Denise Calloway from Paul Jr. High School! *Man, my girl Denise!* Kevin thought to himself.

"Hey, Denise...Denise...Denise..." (she tried to ignore him while holding in a laugh), look at me, Denise...look at me..."

Denise turned suddenly and looked him squarely in the face. "What BOY?!", she said, annoyed. "Shut the hell up!", Kevin whispered to her.

She laughed and hit him on his shoulder. "See...DAMN! What happened to your lip?!

"David", Kevin replied.

Denise looked back, confused. "David? Who, Austin's brother?"

"Nah, my brother", Kevin told her.

"You got a brother?", she asked.

"Yeah, he goes here too. He's in the 10th", Kevin said.

"I never knew you had a brother that goes here. Does he look like you?", she asked.

Kevin looked over at her and smirked. "So, since I don't want your goofy-looking ass, you think you're going to try and crack on my brother? Have some respect for yourself! Damn, Shorty!"

Denise rolled her eyes. "You wish you COULD get with me, with your pressed ass!"

Kevin leaned back in his chair and looked at the ceiling. "I come back here, trying to chill, and somebody always gotta be pressed and shit..."

Denise burst out laughing. "That's 'cause your ass IS pressed!"

"Quiet back there!" Mr. Allen yelled out.

"Yes, sir", Kevin yelled back. They sat quietly for a minute.

"Yes, sir..." Denise said under her breath.

Kevin turned to her. "Denise.... Denise...look at me..."

"SHUT UP!", Denise sneered back.

Kevin turned back and mumbled, "I don't know why I talk to you. Ugly broad. That's why I don't get no play. Sitting around with your balled-up-looking ass all the time."

Denise turned to the desk on her other side. "Hey, Paul! I like that sweater, that looks nice on you. That's your color right there."

Paul smiled. "Thanks, Denise! You're looking good as always, too!"

Denise pretended as if she were blushing. "Thank youuu." She turned back and sat silently for a second and then turned to Kevin. "Your turn."

"Your turn what?", Kevin said.

"DUH, your turn to flirt with somebody in the class. Go ahead. We'll see who the ugly one is", Denise challenged him.

Kevin looked at her. "You serious?"

Denise just stared back.

"Ok." Kevin took a piece of lint from his pocket and tapped Cynthia on her shoulder.

Cynthia Boone was a cheerleader. Stuck up and snobbish. Young gold-digger in the making. My 48-year-old self knows the 80's beat her down, as she got passed around from one drug dealer to the next. Fast money, fast fall.

She turned around. "What?!" She said as if annoyed.

David held up the piece of lint to show her. "I just picked this off your jacket and didn't want you to think I was behind you doing something funny. You always look sharp, and I know you wouldn't want this all over you."

Cynthia smiled the smile she'd probably practiced a million times in her mirror. "Oh, thank you… (as she turned back around looking Kevin up and down with a half sneer) you look nice, too."

"Thanks!" Kevin said as he sat back smiling at Denise.

They sat quietly for a second.

Denise leaned in close to Kevin and whispered, "She jive gritted on you, though", Denise said.

"That's Cynthia Boone, though", Kevin told her.

Denise nodded her head and smiled. "Yeah, …true." She put her hand out to give him 'five.'

Kevin leaned away from her and said, "No, no…I don't want to be seen touching you, because…you know…you're…"

Denise interrupted, "Boy, shut up!"

6th period. Mrs. Alexander was one of Kevin's all-time favorite teachers; she and Mr. Jesse Woods, from Takoma Elementary. They were the only teachers who seemed to really care, and thought Kevin had the potential to be something special, or that he had something special. But then, they made all their students feel that way. As Kevin walked through the door, Mrs. Alexander beamed as usual.

"Kevin! Do you have a story for me?", she asked.

Kevin had forgotten. He'd cut school so much, that he and Mrs. Alexander made a deal. One story or poem a week is what she would grade him on, regardless of attendance. Eight stories and poems were stapled to her chalkboard; three of those were his.

"No, Mrs. Alexander, I'll be sitting in today and from now on", he said.

She stepped back, smiling and feigning amazement. "Oh really! Well, I'm glad to hear that, but you still owe me a story or a poem for this week."

Kevin smiled. "I'll give it to you in about…5 minutes."

Mrs. Alexander smiled. "Ok. Don't hand me some quick junk, though. Have a seat."

"I won't", Kevin replied.

Kevin wrote a lot while he was in the Navy. It was one of the things he used to do when he got bored; and he got bored a lot, too. *How'd that quick one go…?* Kevin thought as he began jotting down his words…

> *Life*
> *The sun on your face*
> *Happy times as a kid*
> *The guilt that you feel for that thing that you did*

The warmth of a hand
A slap in the face
The want in your heart to be some other place
The loved ones you've lost
The dues that you've paid
The lives that you've touched and mistakes that
you'd made
The pain in your back
The creak in your bones
The realization that time marches on
The cold winter's wind
Last embrace from your wife
The beginning, the middle and end of your life.

Kevin walked back up to her desk and handed the poem to his teacher as her students were still taking their seats. Mrs. Alexander placed it on her desk and continued to stand by the door greeting each student with a smile as they walked in. Kevin watched her interacting with the students, studying her face from the back of the room, looking for any air of her demeanor being fake or forced. There was none. Mrs. Alexander looked happy to see each one of her students. He was right, she is special!

As the last student took their seat, Mrs. Alexander returned to her desk, gave out the assignment and picked up the poem. She read it and put it back down.

Damn...the hell was that? Kevin thought.

He was still very sensitive about his writing and how people received it, especially people he admired and looked up too.

She picked up the poem again and her head started slightly bobbing up and down to the rhythm of the sentences in the poem. A slight smile came over her face, then grew bigger. She looked up at Kevin nodding her head, put her thumb out sideways, then raised it up like Caesar and smiled big, almost giddy.

Kevin laughed a laugh of relief, slumped in his chair and grabbed his chest.

"Teacher's got-damn pet..." Kevin heard from the desk two rows over. He knew the voice. Denise again. He sat back up straight and shook his head side to side, looked at the ceiling, and exhaled as if frustrated.

Denise got up and took the seat behind him.

Kevin looked at the ceiling and pretended to pray aloud, *"For God's sake...."*

Denise punched him as she sat down, "Shut up boy!"

Mrs. Alexander arose from her chair and stood at the front of the class, WITH THE POEM IN HER HAND!

Kevin felt his underarms gush sweat, his hands got moist, and his face went flush. NOOOOOOOO!!! He screamed in his head and tried with all his might to convey to his teacher a look that said, *please don't do this!*

She looked at Kevin and gave the 'hush up' sign with her hand and said, "Class, I'd like to read to you a poem." She then proceeded to read the poem aloud. To the class. In front of everyone.

He thought to himself, *"Where, in the hell, is a needle full of heroin when you need it!"*

After what felt like forever. It was over.

Everyone in the class looked at Corliss Little and Tiffany Brown.

"That was nice! You wrote that?" Corliss asked Tiffany.

Tiffany replied, "No I didn't. But that was a good one."

Everyone was looking around as Mrs. Alexander just stood there smiling at Kevin as if he were her child.

"Kevin wrote it." She said.

"Kevin WHO? Not Kevin Allen!" Seemed to be the consensus of the entire got damn class.

"Kevin Allen. One of my best students. Who gave me his blood oath (she said staring directly into his eyes) that he will be attending class regularly in the future. Isn't that right Kevin."

"Yes (Kevin had to clear his throat due to his nerves) Yes mam" he said. "Yes Mam.

"Last embrace from your wife..." Denise whispered to him while cracking up laughing.

Kevin turned his head to the side looking back at her. "The hell Shorty...?"

Denise wiped her eyes. "Damn man I don't know...I would have been embarrassed like hell! I gotta give you some props on that one for real!"

"Damn man I don't know...glug glug glug glug shut the hell up!" Said Kevin mocking her.

Denise slapped Kevin so hard on his neck the whole class turned around.

Kevin played it off as if nothing happened

As everyone turned back he said to her, "I hope when you get married your man beats your ass every got damn day!"

Denise laughed. "Please. Any man hit me, his ass AND mine will be on the front cover of Jet AND Ebony magazine for how I killed his ass!"

Kevin mumbled under his breath, "You foul as shit!"

Denise laughed and then poked Kevin. "Aye man, your little crush Tiffany Brown keeps looking back here at you. What you going to do? You gonna ask her this week or punk out again?"

Kevin had forgotten how close he and Denise were and that he had once confided in her how every Friday he wanted to ask Tiffany for her number so that they could go out. But every Friday he punked out. He'd always felt that Tiffany was probably "The One" and sadly, another one he let get away.

"The hell was I thinking" Kevin thought to himself.

"Why the hell do I talk to you slim…" Kevin said resigned.

Denise sat there quietly for a minute and then said, "I'ma show you why…" Denise got up from her seat, walked over and tapped Tiffany Brown on the shoulder.

"Excuse me Tiffany, do you have an extra pen I can borrow? Mine ran out."

"Yeah girl here" said Tiffany as she pulled a pen from her bag.

Denise took the pen and then she stooped down and began whispering back and forth with Tiffany Brown. Tiffany, during the conversation, turned back and looked at Kevin, and then back at Denise.

"I know you're not over there selling me out like that shorty… playing is playing but damn…" He thought to himself.

Denise scribbled something on her hand and walked back to her seat behind Kevin.

He waited a few seconds and then turned back at Denise with a pissed off look on his face and as he was about to say something, Denise put her finger up to her lips in the "Be quiet" signal and removed it.

"Shut the hell up! That's why!" She said as she held her palm to his face and in it said:

Tiffany Brown, 291-5894 Don't call after 8.

Kevin looked at Denise, smiled big and went to give her a high five. Denise said, "No sir, you ugly, don't touch me. Just copy it down."

"The hell with that!" Kevin looked at her. Got up out of his seat and gave her a big hug.

"Ohhhh damn! (Denise whispered in his ear) You forget your deodorant this morning or something, DAMN Kevin!"

Kevin let her go and stepped back. "I was nervous…"

"Man, go take care of that before you holla at Tiffany damn man here."

She reached in her bag and hands him a roll on. "NOW!"

Kevin looks at it as he takes it before putting it in his pocket.

"Got damn Secret?!" Kevin said as he looked at her.

"That shits better than that fresh peeled onions smell you're working with!" Denise said.

Kevin resigned himself. "Alright, alright shorty. Good looking out for real."

Denise pulled her sweater up over her nose. "Yeah, yeah look out for me, look out for me, go, go!"

"Man it isn't that bad stop faking'"

Denise looked at him seriously. "I'm about to get loud on your ass if you don't go right now for REAL!"

"Aiight, I'm out. Mrs. Alexander I need to go to the bathroom." Kevin said as he walked to the front of the class.

She took the hall pass out of her desk and went to hand it to him. "You're coming back right?"

Kevin just looked at her. "After all that, you're going to give me a hard time?"

She smiled. "I don't see you much so when I do, I've got to mess with you a little. Hurry back."

He took the pass and went in the bathroom, remove his shirt, grabbed some paper towels and began washing his underarms with that nasty white schoolhouse soap.

Just then Dave and Rick, old classmates from Paul, came running in and ran into separate stalls.

As he was pulling his shirt down, Harrison, the school's security/hall monitor came in the door.

"Kevin Allen, what you doing out of class?" Harrison asked.

"Bathroom. Hall Pass." Kevin said flatly.

"Hell, what you doing in class is what I should be asking. Anybody come in here while you were in here?" Said Harrison.

Kevin looked at him. "No sir. Not since I've been here."

"Ok. Get back to class boy." He said as the bathroom door shut behind him.

Kevin straightened his clothes and proceeded to walk out.

As he reached for the door he heard Dave's voice from the stall. "Aye man."

"Yup." Kevin replied as he left the bathroom.

Hell, let them enjoy what little freedom they have. Those two have years of jail time ahead of them he thought to himself.

As he returned the pass to Mrs. Alexander, she looked at his pants and smiled. "Everything okay?" She asked.

Kevin looked down at his pants and saw the water droplets across the front.

"Sink splash." He said.

"I'm just teasing you. Go back and have a seat." She said.

As he was returning to his seat his eyes fell upon Abigail Jenkins. Small little girl. Quiet. He noticed her fingernails. Two had blood around the nails. She constantly bit them all day. He remembered something came out about her being abused. He remembered she killed herself shortly after High School. As he walked by her desk he tapped her.

"Hey Abby…come on shorty…" and as he mimicked biting his nails he gave her a disproving look.

She looked up at him with a look of surprise and shock. And then withered back into her shell. "Ok…"

"You're going to want those hands to look right when that dude slips that ring on your finger when your older right?" Kevin said smiling at her.

Abby smiled timidly. "Yeah, I guess so".

Kevin smiled big at her. "That's what's up shorty!"

As Kevin turned to walk back to his seat he looked toward Mrs. Alexander who was staring at him intently. Seriously. As if she were trying to see through him.

He put his hands up as if in surrender.

"I'm going, I'm going." Said Kevin as he took his seat.

Abby always sat front row in Mrs. Alexander's room right by the door. No one talked to her and she didn't talk to anyone except Mrs. Alexander. Abby never wore what could be considered the latest fashions. Small, and so pale skinned she could almost pass for white. Around her eyes were dark as if she didn't sleep and when Kevin looked into them he could sense pain. He'd always been an empath. It was like a sixth sense with him. He could look into the eyes of anyone and tell if something wasn't right. And it always seemed as if people in pain gravitated toward him as if he were a magnet. As if they could sense that he knew of their pain and somehow felt that he could bring them relief of it. She was pretty though. Her hair was fine and curly but for some reason always looked as if it were wet. She was always overdressed. As if she were trying to hide her figure from the world by wearing ill fitted clothing. Sometimes she'd stay behind after class and her and Mrs. Alexander would talk alone.

Kevin took his seat and Denise says, "So I '
and you start talking to crazy Abby? Th

Kevin leans back in his chair. "You ever tan.

"Hell naw! Don't nobody talk to her. She's crazy
Denise says.

"Hey Fam do me one more favor. A big one. Use some of that
Denise flavor and just talk to her sometimes." Kevin whispered
quietly to her.

"Man, you crazy as hell. Hell naw!" Denise snapped back as
she rolled her eyes.

Kevin turned around and looked at Denise.

"You serious?" Denise said.

"Yeah, for real. Think about how you'd feel if nobody talked to
you. She's just shy." Kevin said.

Denise looked at the ceiling and then back at Kevin. "Yeah ok.
But if her ax murdering ass get me I'ma..."

Kevin interrupted her. "If her ax murdering ass get you you'll
get dead. You kind of dumb aren't you? Don't know how death
works do you?"

Denise looked at Kevin and said loud enough for the class to
hear, "Give me back my Secret!"

Everyone looked back but Kevin played it cool and smiled, "I
ain't gonna say nothing. Don't worry about it." He said.

lass slowly turned back to what they were doing.

nise laughed. "Damn...quick thinking. Hmmmm...Fam uh? Yeah slim, hell yeah, we're Fam!"

They both laughed. The bell rang.

As he passed Mrs. Alexander's desk she said, "Kevin, a quick word with you, please."

She waited until the class left. "What did you say to Abigail?"

"I told her to stop biting her nails," Kevin responded.

"And?" replied Mrs. Alexander.

"I think I said she will want them to look good when her husband proposes to her or something like that" Kevin said.

Mrs. Alexander sat back in her chair with a look of relief. "She was smiling. She rarely does. I hope this isn't your way of teasing her."

"No ma'am. I'm just being nice to her, that's all. I think something is going on with her, and I'm just being nice. That's all." Kevin reassured her.

"Why, did you hear something?" A look of concern washed over her face.

"No, except that everyone thinks she's crazy. I don't, but something's up with her, though," he said. "But she was smiling, that's good. ..."

"That was nice of you, thank you! I'll talk to you later. That poem is going up on the board, too! I loved it!" she said.

"Yeah...Mrs. Alexander, about that..."

She interrupted him. "You're creative, and it's my job to bring that out of you. In fact, you're going to look back on today as the 'good old days' when I read your stories. Before the year is out, you'll be reading them in front of the class yourself, so you'd better get used to talking to groups. I think you have something to say to people. That shyness will be a mental jail for you if you don't overcome it. Come on Kevin, you had to go to the bathroom to clean up after I read your poem. Do you think that's, right?"

Kevin shrugged. "Nope."

"Ok then. We're going to work on you overcoming your shyness. And don't worry, I'll help you," she said.

"Alright. Thanks," Kevin responded as he opened the door to leave the classroom.

"Oh, and Kevin, good luck with Tiffany. I used to see you eyeing her all last year!" she said with a sheepish grin.

Kevin laughed. "You don't miss nothing, do you?"

She laughed. "It's my class. You all are MY kids!" she said smiling.

Kevin looked back at her with a serious look on his face. "I never told you this, but you're one of the best teachers I've ever had, and the things you've taught me have inspired me for years. Thank you."

Her smile turned serious. "Thank you…for years?" she asked.

SHIT! Kevin thought in his head.

"I meant you're an inspiration for me…" he stammered.

She stared at him intently. "Ok, Kevin. You have a good weekend, and I'll see you Monday."

"Yes ma'am. See you Monday," he said as he left.

He walked down the hallway toward his next class. As he turned to enter it, he stopped when he saw Dave talking to Henry as Henry was reaching in his pocket. *Getting chumped again for his money. Something that happened to Henry almost every day of the year.*

Kevin yelled out "Aye, Dave!"

Dave took the money from Henry and started walking toward Kevin. "Aye, good looking out with Harrison, man!" and gave Kevin a slap on his hand.

"Aye, no problem man…but look, Dave…do me a favor man…" Kevin said.

Dave, still smiling, says, "Yeah, what's up?"

Kevin looks at him seriously. "Ya'll lean off Henry man. Dude got it hard enough, you know what I'm saying?"

Dave looked at Kevin surprised. "What, he kin to you or something?"

Kevin laughed. "Nah, man but...look at dude. Shoes rolled over, clothes all old and worn. Dude is poor as hell. Then he comes here and ya'll go at his pockets. Come on, man...even Robin Hood only stole from the rich, right?"

Dave stared at him questioningly.

"Seriously man, dude got it rough enough..." Kevin said.

Dave shook his head up and down slowly. "Alright shorty. But I can only speak for me. I can't stop bamas from hitting him when I ain't around."

Kevin smiled, "Cool man, that's what's up...Soooo, let me get that."

Dave smiled. "Get what?"

Kevin laughed. "That money you just took from him."

Dave said, "What money?"

Kevin just stared blankly at Dave.

Dave sighed, reached in his pocket and put the money in Kevin's hand. "Shorty, we even!"

Kevin laughed. "Nah, I owe you one. Good move man."

Dave shook his head as he walked away and said, "Later man."

Kevin walked up to Henry and handed him his money.

Henry looked at Kevin and said, "You didn't have to do that."

Kevin says, "Sure didn't."

"Then why'd you do it?" Henry asked.

Kevin said, "We're all from Paul and used to be jive tight up there. Some of these dudes got to Coolidge and started acting brand new. I'm still the same dude that you know from Paul. Know what I'm saying?"

Henry smiled. "Well…thanks man."

Kevin started to walk away and then turned back and said, "One fight Henry. That's all you gotta do. Don't even have to win. You just gotta TRY to win. You bust one of these dudes in the mouth one time, and all of them will stop messing with you. I know you stare at your ceiling at night thinking about what you should have done. DO IT! Seriously, a coward really does die a thousand deaths."

Henry just stood there staring at Kevin and then said, "You're right…" Then he turned and walked away. Henry got on drugs bad after graduation. Kevin saw him down on 14th and W, heroin addicts' row, in the late 1980's. Kevin sighed as he watched Henry go around the corner and said to himself, *Come on Henry, you're better than that, man…*

As Kevin turned back toward his classroom, he noticed Mrs. Alexander standing outside her door at the end of the hallway. She NEVER stands outside her class when students are entering. She was looking at him. Kevin waved as he dipped into his class. She didn't wave back. *Gotta be more careful, man...Mrs. Alexander ain't no joke!* he thought to himself.

Kevin walked into the classroom and was met with the same stares he'd received in every other class that day. He shook his head and smiled as he walked to the back row to take his seat, then thought to himself, *What the hell was I thinking back then?*

He looked around the class and then remembered why he cut class so much. A lot of the people there had attended Elementary and Jr. High with him, and were nothing now like who they were then. Many of his classmates were chameleons now, faking to get along, getting in cliques, and assimilating. Everyone trying to look and act as if they had money or were 'well off'.

As Kevin looked at what he had on, he realized that he, too, at that stage of his life, had fallen victim to that idiocy, sporting an Izod sweater, Izod belt, and Izod socks. He shook his head as he picked at the alligator logo on his sweater. *If these folks only knew how many yards I raked and cut. How many neighbor's cars I washed, and how much snow I'd shoveled to get this stuff...I'm some kind of idiot! Making someone else, who already has plenty of money, richer, so that I could LOOK LIKE I had money. How dumb was that?* He shook his head in disbelief and laughed at himself a little.

"You going to practice today?" It was Bruce, cool, down to earth brother that played on the chess team. Bruce was an 'off-brand' kind of dude or 'nerd' type.

The question snapped Kevin out of his '1,000-yard stare'. "Today? yeah, yeah I'm going." Kevin was taught chess by his friends James and Nate's father, who cut no slack to beginners. He was a microbiologist for NIH. Super sharp. The first time they played he'd checkmated Kevin within 5 moves. When Kevin asked for a rematch Mr. Shackelford simply said, "You need to practice more. I'll play you again when you're a little more seasoned." Then got up from the table. That pushed Kevin more than anything to be a become a better Chess player. If that was Mr. Shackelford's intent, he could not have done a better job.

Kevin had 'teams' he considered to be his friends. Bobby and brothers Austin and David, brothers James and Nate, Tony, Tweet, the Watkin's brothers, Fat James, Derrick, Ronnie (The Over the Hill crew) who were his neighbors, Some Lamont-Riggs dudes…he was never at a loss for people to hang or hook school with. Funny thing was a lot of them didn't like each other and the only time they'd be all at the same place was when they were down at the Rec. playing ball.

If Bobby, Austin, and David were hooking school, then Kevin would be with them, usually driving to Catholic schools or Blair and Kennedy high schools in Maryland. If he was with James and Nate, he'd go up to their school, Wilson, and chill, or be in Silver Spring, MD playing pinball or video games at the bowling alley all day. Wilson was a cool school. A lot of the students there had families that had money. He found it odd that the Wilson students, for the most part, didn't dress as well or wear as many designer labels as the poorer kids that attended Coolidge. Austin and David also played on the tennis team with Kevin.

"Ok, good." Bruce said as he took his seat. Bruce was smart, went to college, became an officer in the Army, got married, did the 'happily ever after' thing. He didn't get sucked up in the 1980's drug 'thing' like a lot of people in the room did.

Kevin counted four classmates in the room that died violently in the drug game, and eight that got addicted to crack. There were 12 out of the 28 students in the class that HE knew crack had messed up. Some of the others he never saw after high school, so who knows how they turned out.

Damn... he thought to himself.

Just then, he heard tapping at the back door of the class and looked up to see Austin at the window waving at him to come out. Kevin got up and went outside.

"Aye, shorty we got a cold freak coming over the house!" Austin said.

Kevin remembered this day well. *Lynette from JROTC, and a 'cold freak' she was!*

Kevin looked at his friend disappointedly. "Nah, Austin, I'ma finish out this day. First time in a long time I did a whole day at school. I'll get up with y'all around the way."

Austin looked at Kevin surprised. "Man, as much as you always talk about being in the desert? Alright ya' dry dick bastard, but I'm telling you she's wild as shit! Do EVERYTHING shorty!"

Kevin looked up at the ceiling. He knew! Back then you had to meet the family, be cool with the dog and go with a broad for at least a year then MAYBE she'd blow you.

Lynette did all that off the break!

"Man, fuck you...fuck you...I'll get up with you later." Kevin said laughing.

Austin laughed. "Ok...Alright ya' big faggy. I'll holler at you later."

Kevin looked at him with shock for a second as people walked by them. No one even turned their way when he said it. And it was loud enough for them all to hear. The pre-PC years, he thought to himself. Wild.

"You don't want me to hit it anyway. Once I get that ass, she won't give ya'll no more! Believe THAT shit!" Kevin said.

Austin laughed. "Yeah ok, desert man." As he walked away down the hallway towards the back door. "Later." He yelled.

"Later man..." Kevin replied.

Kevin thought to himself how many times he'd wished he'd done everything differently when he was older. Realizing now how great the pull was to do it just the way he had all those many years ago, hit him hard. "Shit, that freak knew her way around a penis!" he whispered aloud as he went back into the classroom and took his seat with a dejected look on his face.

"Hey, girl." Denise said as Abby was putting books away in her locker.

Abby looked back at Denise with surprise in her eyes. "Uhhhh, hi..." she replied timidly.

"Was Kevin bothering you in Mrs. Alexander's class?" Denise asked.

"No..." Abby said, with a little fear in her voice.

"Oh ok, just tell me if he ever does and I'll make him stop it." Said Denise.

Abby grabbed a book out the locker and closed it. "He wasn't bothering me. Is he your boyfriend?"

Denise reared back. "Who, Kevin?! NO, girl! We're just like... best friends, I guess. Why you ask?"

Abby looked up at her then looked away shyly. "I hear you two back there playing with each other a lot. You sound like boyfriend and girlfriend. If I had a boyfriend, I'd want to have the kind of fun you and Kevin have. That's all..."

Denise looked at her puzzled. "Nah girl, me and Kevin are just cool."

Abby asked. "So, you already have a boyfriend?"

Denise laughed a little. "No, I'm not going with anybody right now."

Abby says, "Oh, ok. Well, I've got to get to class sooo..."

"Ok yeah..., hey, did you write down Lancaster's homework?" Denise asked.

Abby replied, "It's in my locker. I..."

Denise chimes in, "Don't worry about it. I can get it from you after 7th period, ok?"

Abby started walking toward her class. "Ok." She replied as she made her way down the hall.

Damn, that girl is a mess. But she's nice though. She thought me and Kevin?! She is crazy! But she found herself smiling when she thought of Kevin.

The bell rang, and chess practice was over. Kevin didn't feel like he used to on a Friday when school was out. He'd had a good time today, and at SCHOOL of all places! Observing everyone. Knowing how some of their lives would end up, or end PERIOD. Maybe he could steer some away from making those same mistakes? But he remembered there was one that he HAD to save. But, which one?

Kevin walked to the back plaza of the school and sat on the bleachers. He pulled out his notebook and wrote down some of the things he'd wished he had done back then. He raised his head and smiled as he remembered Johnson's car lot over by the Takoma metro station.

Mr. Johnson had a 1970 Torino SCJ Cobra with a 429 that he was willing to sell for 400.00. It needed a new front seat and maybe a transmission, but that joint was forever 'the fish that got away' in his life. "Not this time!" he said aloud as he thought about his money can. *Wonder how much I got?* he thought to himself as he put his notebook away and headed home.

Kevin entered the house, and the first thing he sees is Ellis sitting on the couch. Ellis is his little sister Jean's boyfriend.

He's a little red dude with funny-colored eyes. He never says much. Kind of the 'sneaky' type.

"Aye, Kevin." he says.

Kevin looks over at him with a serious look. "Aye, where's everybody at?" he says.

"Jean's upstairs. David just left about 10 minutes ago." Ellis replied.

Kevin sat down in the chair across from the couch. "Aye man, you can't be up in here when no one else is here. That shit ain't cool."

Before Ellis could reply, Jean comes down the stairs. "Mom said it was ok."

Kevin looked sternly at his sister. "No, Mom didn't say it was got-damned ok! And Dad definitely didn't say that shit was ok!"

Jean looked at Kevin with shock in her eyes. Surprised that he had cursed at her. "I'ma tell Mom you're in here cursing." she said.

"That's cool." said Kevin.

"AND that you've been smoking cigarettes, too." said Jean.

Kevin looked back at her with a blank expression. "That's cool, too. Let's call her now. I'll tell her. But dude ain't going to be up in here when there's nobody home. That shit right there is dead!"

Jean looked at Kevin, surprised that her threats had no effect. Then a resigned look came over her face. "Fine, then. We'll just sit on the patio when nobody's home."

Kevin said, "Yeah, ok." then looked at Ellis. "Seriously man, don't let me or David catch you up in this joint when nobody's home."

As she was walking out the house Jean said under her breath, "Yeah, what are y'all going to do?"

Kevin yelled back as they were leaving. "It won't be good, I can tell you that much!"

Ellis walked out quietly, not making eye contact with Kevin.

The noise was enough to bring Kevin's dog Shadow into the living room. "Ol' Chuck!" Kevin said. The dog was so cool, he gave his dog Shadow the nickname Chuck (after she got 'fixed'). Half-German Shepard, half- whatever jumped over the fence. Loyal and smart as hell. Best dog he'd ever had. Shadow looked at the door close with her ears up and then wagged her tail and came to Kevin.

"Aye, Chuck!" he said as he patted his chest and she jumped up on him.

Dad came home first. He went to the bathroom, then came downstairs, sat on the couch, kicked off his shoes, and started reading the newspaper.

"Hey, Dad!" Kevin said.

His father looked up over the paper. "Hey Kevin, how was school?" That was always his first question.

For once, Kevin felt he didn't have to lie. "It was good. Got another poem put on the wall in English."

His father put the paper down. "How about the rest of your classes? English, Science and Art seem to be the only classes you get good grades in. What about the other ones?"

Kevin said, "I've got some Math and History homework I finished earlier. You want to see it?"

Kevin's father raised his paper again. "We'll see what your report card looks like this semester."

Kevin was just about to ask for his $5.00 allowance when Jean ran in. "Daddy!" she said as she gave him a hug.

His face lit up as he put the paper down. "Hey little girl! How was your day?"

Jean gave her patented sad little girl look. "It was ok," she said.

"What's wrong?" Dad said with concern in his voice.

Jean began, "Well...Jackie's Mom is taking her and Jill ice skating tonight and asked if I could come..." she said sadly.

"Well, how much do you need?" he asked.

"Well, I really didn't want to ask you, because I just went on that field trip at school and that cost a lot..." she said.

"How much, Jean?" he asked as he reached for his wallet in his back pocket.

"It's 10 dollars. But if I eat before I go, then I won't need any money for food when they go to McDonald's afterward," she said.

Dad pulled a few bills from his wallet and counted them before handing them to her. "Go ahead and call Mrs. Harris. Here's 14 dollars. What time will you be back?" he asked.

Jean's eyes lit up as if she didn't know he was going to give it to her. She played Pop like a one-string guitar. Kevin sat back watching her run her game and smiled.

Jean gave her fake disappointed look again and said, "Well…I was wondering if I could spend the night over Jackie's, too. If that's ok?"

"Yeah, that's fine," Dad said. "Thanks Daddy!" Jean exclaimed as she hugged him and bounded up the stairs.

"Well played!" Kevin yelled up behind her.

"Shut up, Kevin!" she yelled back.

"Alright, now!" Dad said toward the steps.

"I mean, be quiet Kevin." Jean yelled back down.

They couldn't say 'shut up' to anyone in the house, and "You're telling a story" took the place of the word "liar" in there, too. Pops was from South Carolina, and was what people called 'old school.'

"Hey Dad, could I get my allowance?" Kevin said sheepishly.

Kevin's Dad took on a serious look. "Did you do your chores?" he asked.

"Yes sir," Kevin replied.

"Your room is clean, clothes put away, dog's been feed, trash taken out, grass cut?" Dad asked.

Kevin looked at him and tried to suppress his smile.

"All done. The grass was cut already. I think David did that," Kevin said.

His Dad leaned slowly to his side to free his wallet while maintaining eye contact with Kevin. "I'd better not find out you didn't do them," he said as he passed Kevin a $5 bill.

"Can I use the car tonight?" Kevin asked.

His Dad looked at him annoyed. "I've got a half a tank of gas in it (as he handed him the keys); you'd better bring it back just the way you found it."

Kevin took the keys and put them in his pocket. "Thanks Dad," he said as he turned toward the stairs to go to his room.

"Find out if your brother needs to go anywhere!" he shouted up to Kevin. "Ok," Kevin said back.

Five dollars! All of that for 5 dollars! I've gotta make some money! Kevin thought to himself as he grabbed some wrinkled clothes from his dresser that he planned to wear tonight. *Maybe*

I'll grab the pick-up and start moving junk for people, or cleaning out their garages and taking stuff to the dump.

I can 'go hard' on selling some signs too. he thought to himself.

Kevin's Dad was a self-employed business owner who had tried to teach him the sign business and how to do lettering. But Kevin had other interests back then. He had done a few windows on 3rd street, including the cleaners and the barber shop, but he didn't stick with it. *There's a couple of joints... SHIT! Johnson's Auto needs new signs! I could do his joint and just trade the job for the Torino! HELL YEAH!* he thought to himself.

He then remembered he had Tiffany Brown's phone number. *Hmmmm...* he thought as he dialed the number.

"Hallo..." answered a young girl's voice. "Hi...can I speak to Tiffany?" Kevin asked.

Kevin had to move the phone from his ear.

"TIFFANY, SOME BOY ON THE PHONE FOR YOU!!!" the little girl yelled at the top of her lungs. "IT'S NOT TONY!" said the little girl.

Kevin could hear fast approaching footsteps in the background and scuffling with the phone receiver.

"Give me the phone!" Tiffany yelled at her sister. "Owww!" the little girl said and then laughed.

Kevin thought to himself, "Tony?! The hell...?"

"Hello," Tiffany said, as if that whole thing didn't just transpire.

"Hey Tiffany, what's up?" Kevin said, acting as if he hadn't just heard all that.

"Nothing. You going to Cynthia's party tonight?" She asked.

"Cynthia who?" Said Kevin.

"Cynthia Boone. Cheerleader Cynthia that lives in Riggs," she said.

"I didn't know about it (and he wouldn't have, either; he wasn't in the "in" cliques at school)."

"Well, yeah. She invited me yesterday. Why don't you see if Austin and David want to come? I think she likes the older one," she said.

"Ok. I'll see what's up. We were supposed to go to something up at Summit Hills. Maybe we can hit Cynthia's later," Kevin replied, not wanting to appear too anxious to see her.

"Cool. I'll see y'all there, then," Tiffany said.

"Alright. Hey, take my number. 291-7679," said Kevin. "Ok, I got it. See you later. Bye."

"Alright. Bye." Kevin took a shower and put his clothes on. "Hey Dad, I'm over Austin's house if David looks for me."

His father looked up from the TV. "You driving over there?" his Dad asked. "No, I'ma walk. Save some gas until we're ready to go." Kevin responded.

"Leave the keys then, just in case." His Father said.

Kevin knew in doing so, David was going to skunk him for the car. Resigned, he put the keys on the table.

"Tell David to come to Austin's house if he has to go out, please." Kevin said.

His father never looked away from the TV. "Ok, leave them there." As he motioned, still not looking up, for him to leave the keys on the table where Kevin had already placed them.

Kevin smiled. "OK…," knowing there was a 100-percent chance that he was going to be a foot soldier that night.

Kevin walked over to Austin's house and rang the doorbell. From inside, he heard Mrs. Grey yell, "Who is it?"

Kevin yelled back, "It's me, Mrs. Grey."

"Come on in, Kevin," she yelled.

Kevin came inside and peeked his head down the steps of the split-level house. "How ya'll doing?" he said, in his 'Eddie Haskell' voice.

"We're fine, Kevin." Mrs. Grey replied.

"They're upstairs," said Mr. Grey.

Kevin went to the top floor of the house and opened the door.

"Close the door man!" Austin said.

They were both smoking cigarettes, with the fan on full blast blowing the smoke out the window.

"Let me get one," said Kevin.

David chimed in, "Isn't NEVER got cigarettes but always trying to smoke!".

"I know the hell you ain't talking!" Kevin said as he grabbed a cigarette from the pack on the table.

"Shorty, you missed it! You MISSED IT!" they both said almost in unison smiling big. "She was over here!"

David chimed in, "We both hit that shit like three times each."

Austin jumped in, "LOOK, LOOK, two hours later the broad called up and said she was in her room playing with herself, thinking about what we did! Cold freak, shorty! You missed it!"

Kevin smiled. He knew. Yup. He missed it. He'd probably miss a lot more good times too. But if missing some good times now meant not spending a winter in that abandominium in Baltimore later, he was cool with that. But DAMN! She *was* a cold freak, though!

"Yeah, yeah, aye man, I probably won't get the Buick tonight. Who's driving?" Kevin said.

David says, "Oh, shit! Let me call got-damn Bobby and make sure he's still coming through."

"Hey, Tiffany Brown said Cynthia is supposed to be throwing something tonight. Y'all trying to go?" Kevin asked.

Austin laughed. "Tiffany Brown? When did you talk to Tiffany Brown?" Austin said as he looked at his brother side-eyed.

"I just got off the phone with her about an hour ago." Kevin said like it was nothing.

"Haaaaaaa!!!" David said. "Your balls finally dropped and you got that number, huh man?!"

Austin looked at Kevin side-eyed. "You ain't talk to no Tiffany. Ain't no way you got your balls up to get that number."

Kevin laughed. "Man, fuck y'all! I got the number!"

Austin looked at him questioningly. "Yeah, how?"

Kevin looked down for a second. "Nah, for real, Denise got the number for me."

Austin and David burst out laughing. "Dude, how you got your girl getting numbers for you! That's some punk-assed shit right there!"

Kevin laughed. "Fuck y'all, that's alright. I got the damn number. Call Bobby, bama's!" He said laughing.

David said, "Oh, now he bucking on us! His balls REALLY dropped! Haaaaaaa!!!"

Kevin looks at them both laughing at him on the bed and thinks to himself, "These two jokers here! These jokers are alright!" and begins to laugh himself.

Bobby finally came through. Late as usual, with his '65 Galaxie 500. He was the only one of the crew that had his own car. Bobby was a natural legal hustler who always had a job. He saved every penny he had, always had money, and was funny as hell too! We turned down 3ʳᵈ St., and Bobby stomped on the gas.

Austin laughed. "You know damn well this thing ain't going over 55, man. I don't even know why you try."

Bobby rubbed the dash. "Come on baby…come on baby…" Sure enough, right around 55 it started losing power.

"Got-dammit!" Bobby yelled as we all burst into laughter.

Kevin wiped the tears from his eyes and, without thinking, said, "Man, change the coil and the cap and rotor."

Bobby looked over and said, "I'm supposed to waste my money on something you say?! Get your Pop's Buick running right, then MAYBE I'll listen to you."

Kevin remembered that wherever they went with the Buick, they had to stay for a while until the car cooled off damn near completely before it started again. *Temp sending switch is bad*, he thought to himself.

"Yeah, whatever man! You'd have to push this thing off a cliff to get this brick to hit past 55!" Kevin said.

Bobby stopped the car at a bus stop. "Should be one here in about 30 minutes. We'll holler at you at the party when you get there. Aye, don't forget to get a transfer, 'cause were hitting

Summit Hills after this one," as he reached across Kevin and opened the passenger door.

"Go 'head with that shit, Bobby!" Austin said from the back laughing. "We just fucking with you, man!"

Bobby pulled off and the door closed itself. "Hahaha...fuck y'all!" he said sarcastically, as he floored it around the corner with one rear tire squealing.

They all laughed at him again.

"Let's hit that Riggs joint first, since it's closer. If it's like that, fuck going all the way out to Summit Hills," Bobby said.

"Nah man, let's hit that Summit Hills joint first," David said.

Bobby looked at Kevin and then into the rear-view mirror at David. "Aiight. We need to 'put in' so we can stop to get some gas first." Bobby looked back at Kevin knowingly.

"Nah, fuck it. Let's go down to Riggs and see what's up with that one first," David said.

Bobby mumbled under his breath. "Yeah, that's what the hell I thought."

Kevin laughed and said, "Yeah, Austin, heads up. Tiffany said the broad Cynthia Boone jive likes you."

Austin comes back, "Why ain't you say that in the first place?! Shit, shorty phat than a motherfucker!"

David laughs. "AUUUUUGGGHHH...

Dry dick-assed Kevin cock-blocking like shit!"

Kevin laughs. "Man, fuck y'all! I just told you didn't I?!" Austin cut in, "Yeah, all late and shit!"

They got to the party, park the car then go around the back and into the basement.

No sooner than all four of them were through the door, Cynthia Boone said, "Hey, Austin…hey, David!". smiling big at Austin and David.

Kevin and Bobby looked at each other, then Bobby leaned in close to Kevin and said, "I guess this broad don't see us, we ghost or something. She probably won't feel it when I grab a handful of her ass later, either. Watch!" He started laughing, leaning on Kevin and punching, like he always has.

Kevin had forgotten about Bobby's way of laughing and cracked up.

That got Cynthia's attention. "Oh, hey y'all…" She said.

Bobby straightened up. "Oh, hey Cynthia." He repeated the same way she said it.

She rolled her eyes and turned back to smiling at Austin.

Kevin and Bobby start making their way into the party.

"Aye man, tap me if you see Tiffany Brown down here."

Bobby looked at Kevin with disapproval. "You still sweating her? Man, let that shit go!"

"Nah, nah, she's the one that told me about the party when I called her earlier. I'm supposed to meet her here."

Bobby looked at Kevin stone-faced. "Yeah, yeah, yeah… when you called her…on the phone, ok." Bobby said sarcastically. "If I see her, I'll point her out…" He said as he made his way deeper into the party.

A short time later, Bobby came dancing over by Kevin and yelled over the music, "I just saw her over by the refrigerator with some cock-diesel bama!"

Kevin stopped dancing. "For real?"

Bobby nodded his head up and down.

"Yeah man, he's crewed up with some Riggs boys. You'd better put two bricks in your pockets before you try to go over there and holler at her!"

Kevin stood on his tiptoes so that he could see her over the crowd. He spotted her with her arms around some guy's neck as he leaned against the wall. *Tony*, he thought to himself., 'Tony' and his crew went outside and after a few records played, Tiffany spotted Kevin and came up to him, dancing, with a sheepish half smile. "Hey, Kevin. I thought y'all were going to go to Summit Hills first. How long you been here?" she said smiling. but kind of nervously.

Kevin played it off. "We just got here a minute ago." Her face lit up. "Oh, ok good!"

Bobby danced by and bumped Kevin. Gave him a head nod and glanced toward the door and said, "Aye."

Kevin saw Tony and his boys coming back inside.

"I'ma go see what's up with Austin upstairs. Smoke a cigarette. I'll be back in a few," Kevin said to Tiffany.

Tiffany nervously looked over Kevin in Tony's direction. "Ok, go ahead and chill. Matter of fact I'll come up in a few myself."

Kevin smirked at her, "Ok, bet", as he walked away.

Bobby followed him outside, through the yard and toward his car. "Damn man, what's up?"

Kevin looked visibly angry. "Isn'tShit, man...," as he paced back and forth. "I can't believe I thought that broad was built out of something! How the hell you going to invite me to a party your got damn boyfriend is at?!" Bobby stood quietly, just listening. "She talking 'bout, 'I thought you were going to Summit Hills first...'" (Kevin said, mimicking a girl's voice).

"Daaaamn...you showed up too early, huh money?" Bobby said sympathetically.

"Yeah, yeah, yeah, I guess so, man." Kevin said as he finally stopped pacing and leaned back on Bobby's car.

"So, what's up man? I got the big bama." Bobby said as he starts hitting Kevin with soft body punches.

Kevin covers up and laughs. "Man go 'head with them big fucked up ashy hands! All you gotta do is scrape him, and he'll bleed the hell out! Nah, I'll handle it Monday! Let's hit the Hills shorty. Fuck this party!"

Bobby looks up and stops swinging. "Bet! Stay here I'ma go grab Austin and David."

Kevin pulls a cigarette out. "That's a bet!" he says as he lights it. Bobby comes back a few minutes later with just David. "Where's Austin?" Kevin asks.

Bobby and David look at each other.

Bobby says, "Austin is busy."

David chimes in, "Yeah, real busy!"

Bobby laughs and leans on David.

Kevin shakes his head smiling. "Let's roll, man!" says Kevin.

"Yeah, we'll come back later and get him." Said Bobby.

They returned to the party a few hours later to find Austin, Cheryl, Tiffany, some 'off-brand' dude, and a few other females sitting out on the back porch talking.

As they walked up, Tiffany puts a disappointed, pouting look on her face. "So, you just left and went up to Summit Hills without saying goodbye, huh?" she said to Kevin with that same sad face his little sister Jean uses.

Bobby leaned over to Kevin and whispered, "DO it, do it now!"

Kevin played it off. "Aye, walk with me for a few…" he said to Tiffany. Tiffany turned to Cynthia and says smiling, "I'll be back in a few."

Cynthia smiled back at her and says, "Alright girl", in that way two girls talk when they share a secret.

Ain't *no secret you dime-neck tricks!* Kevin thought to himself.

"How was the party?" Kevin asked, smiling.

"It was nice, I had a really good time!" she said.

Kevin stopped, pulled out some gum, gave her one, took one for himself, and started walking again.

"Yeah, I jive saw that," he said casually.

"Oh, you did?" she asked happily, not catching what he was inferring.

"Yeah, you and the big dude, Tony, right? All hugged up by the refrigerator. That was Tony, right? Or was that some other boyfriend I don't know about?"

Tiffany stopped in her tracks. BUSTED. "I didn't know he was coming," she said sheepishly.

Kevin stopped too. "Didn't know who was coming? Me or Tony…or whatever his name was."

She looked at the ground embarrassed. "Tony…"

Kevin was feeling it. "Tony? Ok…Tony. Your boyfriend Tony. Tony the dude you go with then, huh? Right?"

Tiffany softly replied, "Yeah…"

"So, Tiffany, how the hell you going to invite me to a party your boyfriend is at? Who does that? And why the hell did you give Denise your number if you already had a boyfriend?"

Tiffany looked up at Kevin and said, "I liked you, and me and Tony haven't been getting along that well. And I was thinking about dumping him, but if you don't want me…."

Kevin smiled. That tone she used. The same tone Jean uses when she's working her magic on Dad. "HELL NAH I DON'T WANT YOU!" Kevin said. "You already showed me what you're about. You ain't loyal, slim. I saw you all hugged up on him looking all in love and shit. That's the same shit you'd do to me with somebody else if we got into an argument! The hell I look like trying to get with a broad that already showed me she ain't loyal off the muscle?! Your girl Cynthia was up in the house with my boy all night. She got a dude that I see drop her off at school a lot. Probably her boyfriend too, right? That's how you and your girl roll, huh shorty? Trying to be players and use dudes like suckers. That's fun for y'all, huh?"

Tiffany shot back at him. "Y'all dudes do it all the time and it's alright, right!?"

Kevin says. "For one, I ain't one of those type dudes, and no, it ain't alright. How is it alright to use people? What's wild is I thought you were different, and you were, I think. But since you got with Cynthia's crew, you're just like all the rest of these fake-assed broads around here."

"Fuck you, then! You ain't all that anyway! Get the hell out of here with that shit! Your broke ass can't do nothing for me anyway!" she said as she began to stomp back toward the party.

"Chase that money shorty! Isn't much different than what prostitutes do!" Kevin yelled back as he began to slowly walk back toward the party.

When he arrived, Cynthia was standing with her hands on her hips and a scowl on her face.

"What did you do to Tiffany?" she barked.

Austin, David, and Bobby stood there with an "Oh shit" look on their faces.

"We talked..." Kevin said as he hit his cigarette, smiling slightly at Cynthia.

"Unh Unh, nah. Ya'll did more than talk for her to come back here looking all upset! What did you say to her?!" she said, still barking.

"We talked... (Kevin took another drag of the cigarette and plucked it in the alley) about Tony," he said dramatically.

"Tony...?" Her voice changed, as if she didn't know what he was talking about. "Tony who?" she said, trying to cover for her girl.

"Yeah, you know, her boyfriend Tony." Kevin said as the other girls on the steps all gave that 'Ohhhhh busted' look at the same time.

Bobby jumped up and clapped his hands. "Welp! It's late, and I gotta go to work tomorrow. Ya'll ready to push?"

Cynthia gritted on Kevin and walked inside to find Tiffany.

"Yeah man, let's roll out," Kevin said.

As Bobby walked by Kevin he whispered, "Good move, man. You see how them ho's stick together. She'd have got you too, if you had messed with her!"

Kevin turned to follow. "Yup." He said as they walked up the alley toward the car.

Austin got in the car smiling. "Well, other than that shit, I got some booty today, AND got my freak on! So, I am got-damned 2-and-0!"

David chimed in, "Well, I got me some today too, so at least I'm 1–and-0." They both sat in the back laughing. "What about y'all? I see Kevin just went 0-and-1! Bobby?"

Bobby adjusted his rear-view mirror so that he could see them. "Fuck both of ya'll faggy dick-eating' bama asses!"

Kevin looked over at Bobby, "Right!"

Bobby laughed and said, "HUH, MAN!"

He dropped Austin and David off first and as they were going up Kevin's street he says, "You alright Champ?"

Kevin sighs. "Yeah man...thought she was built out of something. You know how that goes..."

Bobby drove quietly for a few and then said, "Fuck it, man! Let's grab some beers and hit drunk alley!"

Kevin looked over at Bobby. "That's what's up, man!"

They parked the car on the little road near Takoma pool. Named 'Drunk Alley' because that's where all the Post Office workers came after work to drink beers and throw horseshoes.

Bobby grabbed two Miller's out the bag and passed one to Kevin. He took a long swallow and leaned back in his seat. "These broads man...got-damned sorry as hell, shit! Shorty, you know how I been picking up Allison every morning and driving her to school?"

Kevin looked over. "Yeah..."

Bobby put his head back. "Man...that broad asked me to drop her off at her boyfriend's house on Saturday. All that time I been trying to get with her, she messes around and gets a damn boyfriend! Then has the nerve to ask me to take her to him! Isn't that some shit?!"

Kevin looked over at Bobby who was staring at the car ceiling, popped his beer, took a swig and said, "Bobby, I know you, so what's messed up for real is that I know you took her anyway.

Because no matter what she did to you, you still got feelings for her. THAT'S what's messed up!"

Bobby sat quietly and started looking out the window, then said, "Yup…that shit keeps me up at night. That was some sucker ass shit I did. That's why I pressed you to squash that shit with Tiffany, so you wouldn't wind up like me staring at the got-damned ceiling all night."

Kevin quietly says, "Takers. That's what a lot of folks are, man. Don't care as long as they get theirs. Takers. Givers gotta set limits man, 'because takers don't have any."

Bobby sat up and looked at Kevin. "Got dammit, man, that's some good shit right there! School is doing you alright, huh man?!"

They both laughed.

Kevin says, "You gotta cut Allison back just like I did Tiffany, man. Hard! No explanation, no nothing. Don't need to explain nothing. They know what the hell they did, you know what I'm saying?"

Bobby nods his head. "You right; J6 bus for that ass next week!"

Kevin laughs and then thinks to himself, *Man, Tiffany, I thought all this time you were the one that got away…ain't that some…*

(Bobby interrupts his thoughts) "What's up with your girl Denise? You ain't trying to get with that? She bad as hell, man."

Kevin took another swig. "Nah, man, Denise is a good girl. She's wild out the mouth but…"

(Bobby interrupted him again) "But what? But you already know she's cool? But you already know she's got your back? But she's too pretty? But what man? Huh?"

Kevin laughed. "Yeah, I hear you, but I don't think she digs me like that, you know what I'm saying?"

Bobby swigged his beer and said "Maybe she doesn't dig you like that because she doesn't know you dig her like that, know what I'm saying?"

Kevin looked over at him and laughed. "Dr. Phil up in drunk alley and shit!" Bobby looked at him puzzled. "Who?"

Kevin shook his head. "Nothing man."

Bobby reached for another beer. "Too bad about Tiffany. She phat as hell though…Damn!"

Kevin heard him, but didn't hear him. He was still thinking about what Bobby had said about Denise. *Denise?* he thought. Then he found himself smiling a little when he thought of her.

Kevin awakened to the sound of Saturday morning cartoons. His brother David fixated on the small black-and-white TV.

"What's up, D? You skunked me nice last night for the car," Kevin said.

David spoke without looking toward Kevin. "I went by Austin's house like you told Dad, but y'all had already left."

"Oh ok. What did you get into?" Kevin asked.

David looked back at Kevin. "Why do you care about what I got into?"

Kevin just stared at David.

David turned back to the TV and said, "I took Crystal to the movies."

Kevin thought for a second. "What did Mom do?"

David turned to him puzzled. "What do you mean what did Mom do? She did what Mom does. Listening to the Commodores when I left and still playing it when I got back at 11. Why?"

Kevin says, "I don't know man. Maybe we should take Moms out one day, to get something to eat or to the movies or something…"

David laughed. "Man, you seriously need to get yourself a girlfriend! You gonna take your Mom out?! That's sad as hell."

Kevin just looked at him.

David said, "If you're serious, and I doubt you are, because that ain't you, why don't you just go shopping or grocery shopping with her or something when she goes. Get something to eat then."

Kevin thought about it for a second. "Not a bad idea. You ain't so dumb after all, huh man?"

David replies, "You can look at our report cards four times a year and kind of figure out which one of us is the dumb one."

Kevin threw his pillow at him and it hit him in the back of the head.

David raised his fist in the air and says, "Keep playing man. I'ma bust you in the mouth again!"

Kevin laughed. "You really think you did something, huh man?"

David laughed. "I bet you won't be trying to hug on me in the morning no more. I bet you that!" David said sort of beaming with accomplishment. Kevin laughed out loud. David had never beaten him the four times they had fought. *Let him have it*, he thought to himself. *Good for him!* He jumped out the bed and bumped David on purpose as he passed.

David never looked up from the TV and put his right fist in the air. "You 'bout to get another one of these...keep it up!"

Kevin got dressed and walked down to his boy Shack's house (short for Shackelford). He knocked on the door and one of Shack's little sisters peeped through the window and started yelling, "KEVIN ALLEN'S HERE! KEVIN ALLEN'S HERE!" Their little sisters did the same thing every time, and every time Kevin would laugh.

Big Shack (James) yelled at the door from inside, "Come on in, Kevin."

As Kevin stepped into the kitchen, Nate (James' younger brother) came running down the steps. "JAMES! Where'd you put my tape?!" he yelled at James.

"I didn't have your tape," James replied.

"I saw you with...What's up Kevin? I saw you with it last night," Nate replied.

"Mike had your tape. I didn't have your tape," James said.

Kevin laughed and said, "What tape?"

James says, "Yeah Nate, what tape? The EU or Rare Essence?"

Nate shot back at James, "If you said Mike had it, then how come you don't know what tape I'm talking about?"

James laughed. "EXACTLY! If I had the damn tape I'd know what tape you were talking about! So, what tape?!"

Nate stared at James and started back up the stairs mumbling. "You got my damn tape!"

James looked at Kevin and hunched his shoulders up. "I don't have his tape...no tape. The boy's crazy. What's up Kev?!"

Kevin laughed. "Y'all are always at it, I swear..."

James gave Kevin a look of amazement and said, "It's him! All I did was wake up as a black man again. That's all it takes around here, I guess."

Nate came back down the stairs much calmer. "What's up, Kevin? You trying to go up to Silver Springs?"

James cut in. "App, App...Nate. Did you find your tape?"

Nate, never looking from Kevin's direction says, "Yeah, I found it."

James looked at Nate. Then at Kevin with a *what the hell?* look. Then back at Nate and says, "Well...ok then...apology accepted, I guess."

Nate looks over at James and says, "I still think you had it."

Kevin laughs and adds, 'Hey, let's get a game going. Where's the board at?" In their boredom and to expedite game play, they invented a form of the game Monopoly that they called 'Cut Throat' with million-dollar bills.

James says, "Nah, man I'm trying to do something today. It's nice outside. Let's hit the tracks and go up to Silver Springs for a while. We can play cut throat later."

Kevin says, "Ok, cool."

As James gets up Nate snaps, "Take my belt and my shirt off first."

James slumps his shoulders. "Ok...where's my socks? Are those my socks?" as he points at Nate's feet.

"Come on man, let's just go." Kevin laughs as he gets up.

James and Nate stare at each other for a second, and then James says, "Let's go."

On the way to the tracks, Kevin said, "Let me talk to Johnson real quick."

James laughs. "You trying to get a car from Beat 'em Johnson?" (That's the nickname of Johnson Auto because of the poor shape most of his cars were in).

"Yeah man, I'm getting that Cobra!" Kevin says to James.

"That thing needs a lot of work, man. I would save up for something better. Why don't you get that Granada?" James said.

Kevin looked at the tan, half-vinyl-top car James was referring to and laughed. "A Granada over a Cobra?! You crazy as hell!"

James shot back, "A running car, over a Hooptie! No, YOU crazy as hell!"

Kevin shook his head and thought to himself, *In time, James, in time...*. "Wait right here." He said as he went into Mr. Johnson's office.

Kevin walked in to find Mr. Johnson at his desk. "Hey Mr. Johnson."

Mr. Johnson smiled his used car salesman smile and says, "Hey...hey..." "Kevin" (Kevin interjected).

"Kevin, yeah, how you doing today?" Mr. Johnson asked.

"I'm good, I'm good. I'm still trying to get that Torino across the street from you," Kevin said.

"Well I've got the title in my desk right here. You have the 500?" Mr. Johnson asked.

Kevin smiled. "You told me 400 the last time we talked, though."

Mr. Johnson faked a look of shock. "Four hundred? I had somebody come in the other day and offer me 500, but I told him I was holding it for somebody."

"The other day, huh?" Kevin said smiling.

"Yeah, just this past…what was it Tuesday…Yeah, Tuesday," he said smiling back at Kevin.

The game. Seasoned Used-Car Salesman vs. 16-year-old kid. Except this 16-year-old is 48, Kevin thought to himself.

"I'll tell you what, Mr. Johnson, every sign on your lot looks like it's about to fall in. You've got a 4'x8', two 4'x4', and your door sign, all looking rough. I do signs. My father taught me and owns Metropolitan Signs over on Kennedy Street. How about we make a deal?" Kevin asked.

Mr. Johnson's eyes sparkled a little bit. "What kind of a deal you got for me young man?" he asked smiling.

Kevin took a piece of paper off Mr. Johnson's desk, grabbed a pen, and started jotting down some numbers. He turned the paper to Mr. Johnson when he finished.

"Seven hundred thirty-five dollars?!" Mr. Johnson exclaimed as he laughed. "Nooooooo son, that's way too much money for some signs around here."

Kevin looked at him calmly, took the paper back, and wrote on it again. "I'll give you a $500 credit for the car, which leaves $235 owed. You give me the $235, which really won't cover the cost of supplies, and I get the title as soon as I hang the last sign. Deal?"

Mr. Johnson started rocking back and forth in his chair with his hand on his chin. "How long before I see my signs?" he asked with a serious tone.

"About 10 days, once I get the money," Kevin replied.

Mr. Johnson continues to rock in the chair. "I'll give you a hundred on Monday," he said.

Kevin acted as if he was thinking for a second. "Oh man, I left out the 4'x8' plywood that has to go on the back of the two 4'x4' signs." He scratched out the 235 and put $260 on the paper.

Mr. Johnson looked at the paper, then at Kevin, and said, "Can you get it done if I give you 150 for the deposit?"

Kevin did his best not to act excited, put a look on his face as if he was straining, and said, "Yeah…yeah…I can get it done for $150."

Johnson said, "Good. Come by Monday, and I'll give you the cash." Mr. Johnson extended his hand for a shake.

Kevin calmly accepted the handshake. "I'll write up a receipt for you," he said.

Mr. Johnson responded, "Ok, don't forget…Monday!"

Kevin walked toward the office door and said, "Oh, I won't forget! Thanks!"

Mr. Johnson smiled to himself, thinking *I was going to junk that thing and get 50.00 for it.*

Kevin smiled to himself, thinking *All those signs are going to cost me about 80.00 in supplies, and that car will be worth about $50k when I'm older.*

The best kind of deal is when both parties feel they won in the negotiation on both price and services.

Kevin walked up to James and Nate beaming. "You got it?!" Nate asked.

"Not yet, but I will!" Kevin said, smiling.

James got out of the Granada he was sitting in while waiting for Kevin and closed the door. "Man, this joint is NICE! This is the one you should be buying; you're crazy!" James said to Kevin.

Kevin laughed out loud. "THAT?!" he said pointing at it. "Straight up HOOPTIE!"

James looked at him in disbelief. "HOOPTIE?! You must be smoking that boat or something when you're around Austin and them!"

Kevin, still laughing says, "Yeah ok, man. We'll see who the crazy one is in about 10 years, I guarantee it!"

Sunday morning, Kevin awoke to the smell of bacon and biscuits. It was the one day out of the week that Pops took over the kitchen. His scrambled eggs were still the best Kevin had ever tasted. The call came from the bottom of the steps.

"Okay...wash your hands and come eat," Kevin's dad yelled up the stairs.

Kevin passed his oldest sister Nicole as she came from her room and tried to get into the bathroom first.

"Move, Kevin!" she said as she walked by.

Kevin backed up and let her pass. "Good morning, Nicole... how are you doing?" Kevin asked in a sweet voice.

Nicole pushed by him. "Whatever boy, get out the way!"

Kevin laughed. "I love you..." he said as he stretched his arms out for a hug.

"Boy, you better go on with that. I ain't in the mood for you playing this morning!" as she smiled a little.

"Aww...gimmie a hug, big sister." Kevin said with his eyes half shut kissing at the air.

Over his shoulder, David yelled to Nicole, "Bust him in the mouth like I did, Nicole!"

Nicole laughed and slapped Kevin away. "Go 'head boy, stop playing!" and closed the door behind her.

Jean came up behind him quietly and stood in line for the bathroom. Kevin looked at her and Jean rolled her eyes. "It's like that?" Kevin said to her. "Just leave me alone, Kevin," she said with a perturbed look.

"Alright...alright, dang." Kevin said.

"Bust him in the mouth, Jean," he heard over his shoulder again, and then laughter.

Kevin looked in his room to see David holding his stomach laughing with tears streaming out of his eyes. Kevin started laughing at seeing his brother crack himself up.

"You're having a little too much fun with that, man," Kevin said, which made David laugh even harder.

Kevin shook his head and went back into the hallway to wait for his turn and saw that Jean had slid right up next to the door to take his spot.

Before he could say anything, she looked at him and said, "You got out of line," and smiled.

Kevin looked at her as if about to say something and then resigned himself. "Go ahead, Jean," as he stood behind her.

"That's right, go ahead," she said mockingly.

"Brat!" Kevin mumbled under his breath.

"Stupid!" Jean mumbled back.

After breakfast, Kevin jumped up from his seat and started collecting dishes.

"I'll get the dishes, thanks Dad. That was the best breakfast I've had in a long time!"

Nicole looked at Kevin and said, "You mean like since last week? Y'all need to talk to Kevin. He's acting all crazy!"

Kevin paused in his tracks from yet another slip of the tongue.

"You all leave Kevin alone; maybe one of you should have been doing this all along," Kevin's mom said.

David laughed and mumbled, "Straight up 'Eddie Haskell' move..."

Jean looked at David and laughed. "Right David!" and put out her hand to give him 'five.'

"As long as you two have your hands out, you can go ahead and do rock, paper, scissors to see who does the dinner dishes tonight," Kevin's mom said matter-of-factly.

The smiles, just that quick, were wiped completely from their faces.

Dad laughed a little. *That was kind cool to see* Kevin thought to himself.

After the dishes were done, Kevin went to his room to find David working on a model car.

Without looking up, David said, "That was some sell-out stuff you..."

Kevin interrupted him and asked, "You want the Mustang?".

The 1966 Mustang was a car that their Dad bought for them about a year and a half ago that needed repairs. It was still sitting in the driveway, still not running.

David whipped around in his chair and stared at Kevin intently. "You serious?" He said as if waiting for one of Kevin's stupid pranks.

"Yeah, but you got to help me do some stuff." Kevin said.

David turned back around, said "Nope," and resumed work on his model. Kevin said, "You don't even know what it is."

David said, "It's you, it ain't good, so...nope."

Kevin says, "Man, I just need you to help me make and hang some signs at Johnson's car lot. What's bad about that?"

David turned back around. "That's all...and I get the Mustang?"

Kevin looked at him serious. "That's all."

David paused for a second, thinking. "What do you get out of this, then?" Kevin could barely contain his smile. "Just a 1970 Torino Cobra 429 SCJ..." David's eyes lit up. "Nahhhh! You got that joint for REAL?!"

Kevin laughed. "As soon as I hang the last sign, the title is mine," he said.

"MAN, BET!" David said as he jumped up and they slapped each other 'five' about 5 times.

"When does he need the signs?" David asked.

"In about 10 days," Kevin said.

"SHOOOOT! He's gonna have them in 3! Let's get started on them now, man!"

Kevin laughed as he remembered that David wasn't about procrastinating. You couldn't just come up to him waxing words. Any sentences that start with "I was thinking about...", David was going to get you to do it and do it now! Kevin looked at him and teared up a little bit. *Man, I missed you bro!* he thought to himself.

Tuesday was the day Kevin had to wear his JROTC uniform. That and Thursday's. He joined only because it gave his sorry wardrobe a break. Kevin had three pairs of pants that fit, and made the mistake of buying two of the same type of jeans, on the same day, that made it look like he only had two pairs of pants.

He walked into Mrs. Alexander's class and saw Denise talking to Abby at her desk and laughing. Kevin marched up and did a right face at Abby's desk.

"Let me see those hands!" he said to Abby.

Abby seemed to laugh a little easier as she put both her hands out for him to inspect.

Kevin looked them over like a drill instructor. "Reeeverse Siiiiiyde!" He barked out as he inspected them again. "Very good! As you were!"

He made a left face and continued back to his chair.

Denise leaned in and whispered to Abby, "See, that's why. He's crazy!" And laughed.

"I think he's funny," said Abby.

"Take your seats…" Mrs. Alexander said as she closed the door. Denise came back and sat behind Kevin.

"You corny as hell, man!" she said as she sat down.

Kevin shook his head back and forth, like Bruce Lee when he stomped dude in Enter the Dragon, and said, "Shut the hell uuuuuuuuup!"

Denise slapped him on the neck. Loud, again. Except this time, Mrs. Alexander was looking dead at them. As the class turned around Kevin cuffed his pen and bent down to the floor and acted like he was picking up something. As he sat back up, he held the pen in the air and said, "Sorry, I got it…"

Mrs. Alexander's face went from stern disciplinarian to almost bursting out laughing. She quickly turned to the board and you could see her shoulders shaking a little as she tried to stifle her laugh. She wiped her eyes and turned back toward the class when she got herself together and said, "The assignment is on the board." And took her seat.

"Damn, she was looking dead at me! I was busted!" Denise said.

"You're welcome!" Kevin said.

Class ended, and Abby immediately came back to Denise's desk and started talking.

Kevin looked up to see Mrs. Alexander giving him the "come over here" finger.

Kevin mouthed the words "What'd I do?"

She shook her head no and just kept waving that finger.

Kevin approached her desk and she said, "Stand right here." As Kevin watched the class empty, Abby and Denise quickly scooted by him.

Kevin looked at Denise and said, "Thanks!"

She looked back as she passed and mouthed the words, "I'm sorry," and put on a sad face.

Mrs. Alexander closed the door when the last student left. "You two…" She said shaking her head back and forth. "I don't know if I'll be able to put up with you two every day, Mr. Allen…"

Kevin looked down at the floor. "We'll stop playing in your class. I'll talk to her," Kevin said.

"Yes, it looks like you already did talk to her. You've got her talking to Abby. Abby tells me they studied together at the library Friday." She spoke and looked at Kevin as if she were trying to get a read on him. "Why the sudden interest in Abby, Mr. Allen?" she said, as if she knew something.

"If I told you, you wouldn't believe me," he said.

She laughed and replied "Oh, you would be amazed at the things I believe now."

The way she said that had him wondering what she meant.

Now it was Kevin's turn to look at Mrs. Alexander to try and figure her out.

He thought to himself, *To hell with it*, and said, "I just don't want to burn any (and put a long emphasis on) B r I d g e s. You know what I mean?"

Mrs. Alexander's face gave her away. She knew. Kevin could feel it. She stared at him for a few seconds and then almost imperceptibly started nodding her head up and down. She took a piece of paper from her desk, tore it in half, and wrote on it. She handed it to him. "This is my home number, call me after 7, we need to talk," she said in a serious voice.

Kevin took the paper and put it in his uniform coat inside pocket. "Ok…"

As he turned to go to the door, Mrs. Alexander asked, "How old are you, Kevin?"

Kevin stopped. "You wouldn't believe that either, trust me."

Mrs. Alexander says, "Ok…how old do you think I am?"

Kevin turned back and looked at her closely. "I'd say about 32-34, maybe. Right?" He turned back and pushed the door handle.

"53" she said.

Kevin stopped. "What?!"

"I'm 53, Kevin. Yes, 53. So again, how old are you?"

Kevin turned back around and looked at her, wondering if he should tell her, wondering if it may get him in trouble with Bridges and, if so, then what that trouble might be. But he trusted Mrs. Alexander.

Kevin looked her dead in the eyes and said "I'm 48."

She didn't flinch or show any signs of surprise. She simply said, "Make sure you call me."

"Ok," he said as he walked out the door.

Denise and Abby were waiting for him on the other side. "Did you get in trouble?" they both said, almost at the same time.

Kevin smiled slightly. "Nah, but we've got to stop playing so much in there. I don't think she'll just let it go next time."

Denise says, "Whew...ok cool."

As all three of us walked down the hallway, Denise asked, "So what happened with Tiffany? I noticed you two didn't say anything to each other or even look at each other through the whole period."

Kevin sighed, "Found out she had a boyfriend."

Again, in unison, Abby and Denise said, "What?"

Kevin laughed. "What are y'all, Siamese twin's separated at birth or something?"

Denise looked concerned. "Awwwww Kev...I'm sorry. I know how you felt about her. Now I feel bad getting her number for you."

Kevin looked at Denise. "Nah, shorty that was some good looking out. That ain't on you, that's on her. Why the hell did she give you the number if she had a boyfriend?! Who does that crap? I can't stand a disloyal broad! Even if she cheats and leaves him for me, then what the hell did I win, a cheater?! To hell with that; I'd rather date a damn nun!"

Abby bumped Denise purposely with her hips and looked at her smiling all big. Denise sighed and looked at the ceiling.

"What the hell was that?" Kevin said as Abby attempted to cover her obvious grin behind her book.

"Nothing!" Denise said as she gave Abby a serious glance. "Abby had too much sugar today! Come on, girl!"

Abby laughed as Denise grabbed her and led her away down the hallway by her arm.

Kevin watched them as they disappeared down the hallway. He thought to himself, *They're getting along good, and Denise IS bad as hell.*

Damn... He shook his head and walked into his last-period class.

Kevin got home, hung up his uniform, put on some shorts, and started doing his homework on his bed. He heard the front door open and close, and heavy footsteps ascend the stairs. He looked up to see his father stop at the doorway and do a double-take.

"Haven't seen you do that since 6th grade. Keep it up, Kevin." He smiled at Kevin.

Kevin knew he hadn't given his dad a reason to smile at him in a long time. "Hey, Dad," Kevin said. And then he remembered. "Hey, Dad!"

His father stopped and gave a look like *"here we go"* and said, "Yeah Kevin, what is it?"

Kevin came to his feet. "I've got a sign job I have to get out in about nine days, and me and David might need your help."

Kevin's father's eyes lit up. All it seemed he ever wanted was to teach them the business, the family business of making signs. He wanted his kids to have a skill to fall back on if times get rough or, in his highest hopes, they grew up and wanted to take over the business in his old age.

"Where. Who?" he said a little excitedly.

"Johnson's Auto, over by the Metro," Kevin said.

His father looked at him with surprise. "You sold a sign to Johnson?" as he smiled big. "You must be one heck of a salesman!" he said as he laughed.

"Yeah, but there's a catch. I'm only getting $260 cash for a 4'x8', two 4'x4's, and a door window," Kevin said.

Kevin's father looked at him puzzled. "All that for 260? You didn't already take the job, did you?" he said disapprovingly.

"Yeah, he gave me the money yesterday. But the deal is, I also get a car, and I'm giving David my half of the Mustang."

Kevin's father looked up at the ceiling and back at Kevin. "Does the car even run, Kevin?" he asked dejected. "You two already have that Mustang that's been in the driveway for a year and a half that hasn't moved."

Kevin looked as optimistic as he could. "It runs…rough though. The transmission slips, and the driver's seat bracket needs to be welded back. But the car is nice."

His father gave 'that stare' again. "Where are you going to keep it, Kevin?"

Kevin thought for a second and said, "Mr. Lucas said David and I could keep the Mustang in his garage this winter to work on it. I'm going to ask him if I can keep the Torino in there instead."

Kevin's dad said, "Got it all figured out, huh?" and shakes his head back and forth while looking at the floor smiling.

"Always!" Kevin said.

That made his dad laugh out loud. "Ok, get your layout together. Here, I've got three sheets of aluminum you can use; what else do you need?" he asked.

"A 4'x8' plywood board cut down to two 4'x4's," Kevin replied.

"Ok, I'll get Braxton to grab that from Hechinger's tomorrow. Anything else?" his Dad asks.

Kevin laughs. "Yeah, some skill."

His father laughs. "Don't worry about that, we'll get that together over time."

Kevin reached out and shook his father's hand. "Thanks, Dad." His father smiled big as he shook his son's hand. "No problem, son. Now finish that homework."

"Yessir!" Kevin responded.

Kevin went back to the bed, stared at his opened book, and thought to himself, *You gotta be kidding me! THAT'S all I had to do for me and Dad to be cooler? Gaaaaaadamn!* He shook his head and laughed as he started back in on his homework.

"See, I told you!" Abby said across the table.

"Shhhhhhhh!" Denise said back to her as she placed her finger over Abby's mouth.

"Stop it! You know you like him!" Abby said smiling at Denise.

"Yeah. I like him. As a friend. Ok?" said Denise frustrated.

Abby kept coming at her. "He's got morals…as much as you were worried about how much he liked Tiffany, he stopped messing with her when he found out she had a boyfriend, right?"

Denise collapsed her arms out in front of her and put her chin on the table and stared at Abby. "Will you please stop it?" she said, frustrated.

"Come on, Denise," Abby said.

Denise pulled herself up, looked at the ceiling, licked her lips, then looked at Abby and said, "Ok, I was surprised that he didn't try to keep talking to her, even after finding out she had a boyfriend. I didn't think he cared where he got some from, as long as he got some. I'll give you that, OK?"

Abby giggled and said, "OK, then," and picked up her book and started reading. After a few seconds, she said from behind the book, "Hey Denise…"

Denise let her book fall forward on the desk and slumped back in her chair and said, "What?! What now Abby, WHAT?!"

Abby looked over her book then closed it, gently placed it on the table, smiled, looked Denise in her eyes, and said, "I noticed you didn't respond to my saying that you were worried about how much he liked Tiffany."

"AND?!" said Denise, frustrated.

"AND, were you?" Abby replied.

Tiffany looked at Abby, smiling a little, and said, "You think you're soooo damn smart, don't you?"

Abby smiled back. "I AM smart. So are you. That's why you should make a move before another Tiffany comes along. Or, don't worry… we two, smart, single girls can come to the library every day and have these great talks!" Abby smiled at Denise with a big, giant, silly smile.

Denise looked at her with a straight face. "Why do I talk to you?" she asked, resigned.

"Because I'm right!" Abby retorted.

"Hello," a woman's voice on the other end of the phone said.

"Hello, can I speak to Mrs. Alexander?" Kevin said. "Kevin?" she asked.

"Yes," he replied.

"This is she, let me call you right back, ok?"

"Yes Ma'am," Kevin said and hung up. Kevin thought to himself, *I wonder how this will go? MAN, I dread this conversation! If she…*

The phone rings, and Kevin exhaled deeply and answered. "Hello."

"Kevin?"

"Yes ma'am," Followed by a loud silence for a second.

"Well, where do we start?" Mrs. Alexander said.

Kevin laughed. "Ladies before gentlemen," he quipped.

He hears her exhale. "Ok...In 1984...I was in a bad place... mentally. I was staying at the House of Ruth Women's Shelter after having been released from a hospital stay after I had been beaten, again I should add, by my then-husband. They gave me a full bottle of Vicodin for my pain and, well anyway...it was there that I met Bridges...are you still with me?" she asked.

"Right with you," Kevin said.

"Whew, that's a relief! Well ok, anyway... he explained to me that someone, I guess, had not fulfilled their destiny and that for things to progress as they should, I guess, that I had to 'DO' something. The next thing I knew is that I woke up the next day and I was back in the DC Teacher's College and it was 1971. It was there that I'd met my husband. The second time I made sure that I didn't meet him again!"

Kevin dropped in. "Yeah, I saw my first ex-wife up at Coolidge the second day I was back."

"What did you do?" she asked.

"I let her walk right on by and didn't say a thing. That's the way I'm going to keep it, too!" Kevin said.

"Bad...?" she asked.

"No, not that bad. But she was like, everything to me. Seriously messed me up. You know?" he said.

"Yeah, I know." She hesitated for a while. "So, tell me…what's your story?" Kevin recanted his meeting with Bridges from beginning to end to her. "Wow," she said.

"Yeah, pretty much," Kevin said.

She hesitated briefly. "So, who do you think it is that you're here to save?" she asked.

"I'm pretty sure it's Abby," he replied.

"What happened to Abby?" She asked with fear in her voice.

Kevin paused. "It wasn't good…" he said. "She was being badly abused by her father, and a few years after High School she kind of…did what we were trying to do before Bridges stepped in."

"Ohhhhh Nooooooo…poor baby…she was so sweet…" she said.

Kevin dropped in, "Well fortunately, she's STILL sweet and I've got to figure out a way to help her."

"I stayed in touch with her after she graduated and then suddenly I couldn't get through to her. I'd leave messages…. with her father…Ohhhhh Nooooooo… that she never answered," she said.

Kevin could hear the sorrow in her voice. "Yeah, don't worry about it, we got her this time!" he said.

"Yes, we do. And I'm going to do whatever it takes for her to get through this time," she said. "I'll talk to you some more soon, Kevin. Good night."

Kevin said, "Good night, Mrs. Alexander...OH HOLD ON...I have a question. How do you feel dating people in their 30's and you're in your 50's? I'm 48 and I'm having a problem wrapping my head around dating girls my age, I mean my new age. You know what I mean?"

Mrs. Alexander laughed. "Well Kevin, you'd better get used to it. You're 16. What are you going to do, try and date 48year-old women as a 16-year-old boy? I'm 33; 33! I'm not going to be dating some 60-year-old man!"

Kevin laughed. "I see what you're saying. Sixteen it is, then!"

"Good night, Kevin. We'll talk some more later." And she hung up the phone.

He felt bad for Mrs. Alexander. She was such a compassionate, great lady. He didn't want to tell her that he was sent back as a back-up because SHE didn't complete her mission the first time as the 'Plan A.' Nope, he thought. He'd never tell her that.

Kevin entered homeroom still thinking about the conversation with Mrs. Alexander from the previous night, and saw Denise once again sitting in the chair behind his. He slung his books down and slumped into his chair.

Denise says, "Hey ugly!"

Kevin simply replied, "Hey fam!"

Denise shoved him slightly in the back. "What's wrong with you?!" she said playfully, but with concern in her voice also.

"Nothing…nothing I'm cool," he said.

She leaned back in her chair, folded her arms and sat silently for a few moments. Then something compelled her to ask, "What, you still tripping off Tiffany?"

Kevin sat up and turned to her with a puzzled look on his face and said, "What? Tiffany? NO! What makes you think THAT?! What the hell you so mad about?" he said as he noticed she was sitting with her arms crossed and lips pursed.

Denise looked away and said, "Nothing. It's just, you come in here looking like somebody killed your dog and you ain't trying to talk, so I just figured you were still upset about your girl, that's all."

Kevin smiled a little and thought to himself, *She's jealous! Haaaaaaa!!!*

He'd been through this enough times in his life, that's for sure.

Let me get my buddy back up, he thought to himself, and said, "To hell with some got-damned Tiffany! That shit is done, fam. I wouldn't mess with her if she begged me!"

Denise smiled a little and teased him, "Awwwww…I thought she was your special boo-boo… The way you were 'pressed' for her all last year… it must hurt, huh?" she said to Kevin, making a sad face.

Kevin turned his head to the side and said over his shoulder, "Shorty…that is so…fucked…up…"

She laughed and sat up and rubbed his shoulder with her right hand in a small, soft circular motion and said, 'It'll be ok, Kevin Wevin," in a child's voice.

"You ain't 'bout shit, slim," Kevin said, as Denise leaned back laughing at him.

She straightened up after a while and bumped the back of his chair with her foot. 'You're gonna tell me what's wrong though, I bet you that much," she said sternly.

Kevin leaned his head back, looked at the ceiling, exhaled, and slumped his head back down. "Shit, alright. Meet me on the back Plaza at lunch, then."

Denise said, "Me and Abby are supposed to be going up to Eatmore's for lunch…"

Kevin turned around. "Ok, well?... Just call me tonight." Denise said.

Kevin looked at her quizzically. "With what number?"

Denise smiled and says, "Damn, that's right…Wow. Long as we've known each other, we never got each other's number! That's crazy...." She started writing her number down on a piece of paper.

Kevin chimed in. "Naw it ain't! You were skinny and ugly as hell! Don't nobody want your got-damned number!"

Denise hit him on his shoulder and laughed. "Yeah well, I'm not skinny anymore, and I damn sure ain't ugly!" she said confidently.

Kevin thought to himself, *You damn sure ain't!*, but said, "You keep messing with that Eatmore's, and Im'ma be calling you got-damned 'Lumpy' by next year!"

Denise smacked his head and went to hand him the number.

Kevin looked around like he was doing a drug deal and said, "Put that shit down! Slip it to me...I don't want nobody to see that..."

He felt a crumpled piece of paper hit his shoulder and roll down his chest and laughed. He wrote his number down while laughing and handed it to her. "Here Denise..." he said.

She took it and put it between the pages in one of her books. "Don't be calling me after 8:30!" she said. "You going to the game?" she asked.

"What game?" Kevin shot back.

"The Homecoming game! We play Wilson today, stupid...you going?" Kevin laughed. He remembered that game well. It was the one when he, Austin, David, and Bobby went down onto the field and started dancing with Wilson's cheerleaders. Coolidge's band was cranking Holy Ghost or something. That was wild as hell. Kevin paused for a minute, thinking.

"You going or not?" Denise asked.

"Yeah…yeah I'm going." Kevin thought to himself, *Hell yeah, I'm going*!

Later that evening. Kevin called Denise.

"Hello, Could I speak to Denise please?" Kevin asks.

"Who is this?" a young boy asked.

"Could you tell her it's Kevin from school?"

"Ok, hold on." He said.

Kevin moved the receiver from his ear because he knew what was coming next.

"DENISE!!! TELEPHONE! IT'S SOME BOY!" the boy said.

Kevin could hear Denise yell back. "Tell him to hold on. I'll be there in a second."

The boy said. "She's in the bathroom taking a shower, so hold on."

Kevin laughed and said, "Ok."

He could hear Denise enter the room, and the boy said, "Ewwwwww…"

Denise shot back at him. "GET OUT, TREY! AND CLOSE THE DOOR!"

Kevin could hear the boy's laughter as he left the room.

"Hello?" she said.

"Hello? You said that like you don't know who this is; like you got other dudes calling you or something! You know who this is! Don't even try me with some got-damned 'hello!' Haaaaaaa!!!" Kevin said, laughing.

"You stupid. What's up? Her voice suddenly got excited and high-pitched. NAH! What was up with you, Austin, and them?! Y'all wild as hell! That was funny as hell, man! Who does that crap?!" she said, laughing.

"Does what?" Kevin asked, as if he didn't know what she was talking about.

"Who goes down on the field and starts dancing with the other team's cheerleaders?! I gotta give it to y'all, that was hype!" she said.

Kevin laughed. "That was Austin who started all that! Dude is wild as hell, I'm telling you!"

Denise laughed. "That's the most fun I ever had at a football game, EVER!" Kevin settled down and said, "Yeah, that was cool."

Denise then said, "Yeah, don't think I didn't see you flirting with that cheerleader, either. She was waiting to talk to you after the game too, what happened?"

Kevin laughed and said, "I punked out again." As soon as he said it, he thought, *SHIT!*

Denise said, "Again? You know her or something?"

Kevin thought quickly. "Nah, I mean, like the whole Tiffany thing."

Denise sighed. "Yeah, 'ol scared-assed Kevin…"

Kevin said, "Yeah, pretty much," and laughed, glad that he had dodged another slip up.

Denise said, "That's too bad. She was real pretty, too."

Kevin said, "Yeah, but you know, red-bone, long hair, light-colored eyes…trouble!"

Denise laughed. "That's not true," she said.

"It is for me," he said. *SHIT! Did it again!* he thought to himself.

Denise said, "With who? Tiffany wasn't light-skinned."

Kevin once again thought quickly. "Nah, not her. I just see the problems Austin and David have with those types of broads."

Denise said, "Oh, but all of them aren't like that, though."

Kevin said, "No, not all of nothing is the same, but I will say a lot of them are."

Denise paused and asked, "So what kind of girls do you like?"

"Loyal," he replied.

"You're still tripping off Tiffany. I'm talking about looks," she said.

Kevin thought hard for a second and said, "My 'perfect' girl?"

Denise said, "Yeah, your perfect girl..."

Kevin paused and said, "5'8" to 6', copper-toned to brown-skinned, athletic build, patient, great sense of humor, pretty eyes, easy smile, smart, and LOYAL!" he said with emphasis.

"You and that LOYAL!" Denise said.

"Ok. And what's your flavor?" Kevin asked.

Denise said, "My flavor, huh? You be coming up with some good stuff...Ok...6'2"-6'5"..."

Kevin interrupted and said, "Check!"

Denise laughed. "Check?! Man please! Anyway, MUSCULAR BUILD! Kevin laughed. "Oh, for real? Ok!"

"ANYWAY!" Denise said, laughing as she went on. "Smart, cute, CONFIDENT, great sense of humor, medium complexion, great smile, compassionate, and, oh yeah, LOYAL!"

Kevin laughed. "See, I got you on that loyal kick now!"

They both laughed and Denise said, "So I guess I'm not your 'flavor' as you say, huh?"

Kevin had to think hard on this one. This was going to be either the start of something with Denise, or possibly the death of it.

"Yeah, I guess not. Your kind of dumb," Kevin said.

"I am hardly dumb! I've been on the Honor Roll since 3rd grade and counting," Denise said. Kevin paused. "That's true...but you're not loyal."

Denise said, "That's one thing I don't even play with."

Kevin took the step.

"So, you're smart and loyal, huh? OK," he said.

"OK what?" Denise asked sharply.

"I said OK! You sure you're not stupid?" Kevin asked.

A smile slowly spread across Denise's face, and she said, "Oh...ok."

Kevin said, "So?"

"So, what?" Denise replied.

"So, what about me? Am I your flavor?" he asked.

Denise laughed. "Are you MUSCULAR?!" And burst out laughing.

Kevin laughed and said, "I just stepped off the curb, ain't even look both ways. Never saw that bus coming. Damn!"

Denise came down from laughing and said, "Nah, for real, you're alright." Kevin laughed. "Got-damned ALRIGHT! What the hell is that?!"

Denise replied, "I guess it's the same as some got-damned OK!"

Kevin tried to make his voice sound sexy and said, "Oh, for real...you still naked out of that shower?"

Denise said in a sexy voice, "Nah baby, but if you call Tiffany up I'm sure she's probably naked with some dude somewhere. Maybe you can get next."

Kevin was silent for a moment and then laughed. "Well played..."

Denise said, "Hungry ass...."

Kevin said, "I was just jiving, damn!"

"Right! Sure, you were just jiving...anyway, what were you so upset about today?" She said.

Kevin said, "You're gonna think I'm lying, but I can't even remember what it was after you did that sexy voice thing, for real. Damn! Wasn't expecting that..." Kevin laughed.

"Nah, don't even try it. Remember, I'm old, ugly, skinny Denise, right?"

Kevin laughed. "Yeah...it's getting harder and harder to joke you like that, trust me. And, sorry 'bout that."

"Sorry 'bout what?" Denise asked.

"I know you're over there blushing like hell. My bad."

Denise laughed. "Boy ain't nobody over here blushing because of you!" Denise was smiling big, and blushing.

"Alright, Alright…shorty I gotta get off this phone and get some dinner. I'll holler at you tomorrow," Kevin said.

"Ok, I gotta go too. Bye."

"Hey, Denise," Kevin said.

"What?" she replied.

"Denise." "What, Kevin?"

"Say goodbye in your sexy voice for me…"

Denise laughed, said "BYE, BOY!" and hung up the phone.

Kevin moved the receiver from his face and stared at it. *What the hell just happened?* he thought to himself.

Denise sat on her bed quietly, slowly rocking back and forth, staring at the phone. She thought about the conversation she just had and felt, for the second time in her life, butterflies in her stomach. The first time was in the 7th grade. *"What are you doing, girl?"* she said aloud to herself.

"Hey David, thanks for helping me with those signs, man," (Kevin said as he extended his hand to David with dollar bills in it. "I appreciate that. Good looking out!"

David looked up from under the hood of the Mustang and said, "What's this?"

Kevin said, "Something for you, for helping me."

David said, "I thought the deal was I help you and get your half of the Mustang? You ain't gotta give me no money. I'm cool with our deal."

Kevin said, "I know, just take it. Take Crystal out, or get a starter for this so we can get it going. I'll help you drop it in."

David looked at Kevin's hand. "You sure, man?"

Kevin laughed. "Hell, yeah! I'ma probably need your help pulling that big-assed C-6 out of the Torino if it's really bad."

David took the money and put it in his pocket. "I got you! You think it's the starter huh?"

Kevin said, "It's actually the starter solenoid, but you may as well get a whole new starter. At least then you'll know what you've got."

"Yeah, that's true," David responded.

Kevin reached back in his pocket and pulled out a 10-dollar bill.

"Hey, grab a temperature sensor switch for Dad's car too, while you're there."

David took the money. "So, you're just Mr. Hot Rod magazine now, huh?"

Kevin laughed.

In his first life, he graduated from auto mechanic school after he dropped out of Coolidge, and worked for Bob Banning Dodge until they folded. Then he had joined the Navy.

"Something like that," he said.

"Where's the Cobra?" David asked.

Kevin smiled. "THE COBRA! Man, I like that! Johnson had it towed to Mr. Lucas's garage yesterday. I'ma go check it out later."

David said, "You're a trip! I'll go with you when you go."

David paused and went into his country voice impression. "What you gonna do with that pocket full of money, pimpin'?!"

Kevin laughed and thought about it. "Phyllis Hyman is supposed to be up at Blues Alley next month; I think I'll buy two tickets and have Dad take Mom to that show."

David looked at Kevin confused. "What? You gonna do what? And you know Dad ain't trying to go out nowhere anyway."

Kevin laughed and said, "I'll say the tickets are from all of us, and I'll have Jean give them the tickets. Dad will do it then."

David thought for a second. "You right about that! See what all that school is doing for you? You ain't as dumb as I thought you were!"

Kevin laughed and said, "Whatever man, later."

"Alright, later. Thanks Kevin man!" David replied.

No problem, bruh!" Kevin said as he walked away.

He thought to himself, *Ol' David! One of the nicest dudes I ever knew. Great brother and a great father. Died way too soon...*

Kevin called Denise. "Hello?" he heard her say.

"Say it sexy," he replied.

"You're stupid! What's up?" Denise said.

"Aye, let's do something," Kevin said.

"Something like what?" Denise said back, in a way that seemed as if she thought he was hinting at sex.

"I don't know. Walk. Hit the park. Something, you know?" Kevin said.

"Ok. I can only stay out for maybe two hours though, so I guess we can meet somewhere halfway," Denise said.

"Nah, I'll come by and get you," Kevin said.

"Why can't we just meet?" Denise asked.

"Nah, I don't like the idea of you out there walking by yourself. It's getting late."

Denise laughed. "Awwwwwww..." she said.

"Seriously?" Kevin said back.

"Ok, ok. That WAS sweet, though," Denise replied.

Kevin laughed. "Shut up. Where do you live?"

Denise gave Kevin her address.

"Hey Ma, I'm going out for a while. You want me to bring you anything back?" Kevin asked.

His mother smiled and said, "I can't think of anything. How long are you going to be, and where are you going?"

"Down by the park for a minute to meet a friend."

"No, I don't need anything. Be back before it gets too late, and be careful." she said.

"I will," Kevin said as he kissed his mom on the cheek and hugged her. "Oh, so you have your cologne on...hmmmm..." she said smiling.

"Yeah Mom, it's a girl I'm going to see," Kevin said.

David yelled from the next room, "'Bout time!"

Kevin shot back, "Man, shut up!"

Kevin's mom said, "Alright, you two..."

Kevin looked at her smiling, "That didn't deserve a shut up? Ok. Be quiet, David. Jeez!"

Kevin knocked on Denise's door. The door opened and a little boy said, "Hello?"

Denise popped him on his hand and said, "How many times have I told you not to open this door?!"

The boy's face slowly saddened as if he were about to cry.

Kevin said, "What's up, little man? What's that on your shirt?" and pointed his finger at him.

"Where?" the boy said.

"Right there," Kevin said as he poked him in the stomach. "Where?" the boy said.

"Right there," Kevin said as he started tickling him. The boy laughed.

Kevin said, "Hey man, you can't answer the door like that, because there might be a bad guy outside trying to get in and hurt you, ok?"

The boy looked at him and said, "Ok."

Kevin grabbed his hand and shook it. "Good man, good man!"

The boy smiled and ran into the next room. Denise looked at Kevin with surprise.

"What? I've got a little sister. I speak fluent kid," Kevin said.

Denise shook her head back and forth. "Just surprise after surprise after surprise with you, huh Kevin?" as she grabbed her windbreaker.

"Mom, I'm leaving," she yelled into the house.

"Hold on, Denise," an older woman's voice responded. "I need to see who you're leaving with, so I know who to look for if you don't get back in time."

Kevin looked at Denise wide-eyed.

"How are you doing, Mrs. Callaway?" Kevin asked as she came to the door. "Is this the boy from school, Denise?" she asked.

Denise looked at her mom, seeming shocked and surprised, and thinking to herself, *I know you're not doing this*, and said, 'Yes Mom, this is Kevin."

Her mom said, "Ok. I just wanted to lay my eyes on him. He's kind of cute Denise, huh?"

Denise just stared at her mom with her mouth half open. Her mom laughed. "Ok ok, y'all go and get back on time. Nice meeting you, Kevin."

"Thanks, and nice meeting you too, ma'am," Kevin said.

As they got a few feet away from the house, Kevin said, "I could have stayed there all day watching you squirm. That was hilarious!"

Denise laughed. "Mom's always trying to embarrass me, I swear."

Kevin said, "That's their job. I guess it's payback for changing all those dirty diapers or something."

Denise said, "Yeah, that and the fact that she's really over-protective of me because of my big sister Catherine."

Kevin asked, "What's up with her?"

Denise looked saddened and said, "She went to a party with some friends two years ago, and someone put something in her drink. She kind of doesn't function well anymore. We have to dress her now and help her with other stuff. It kind of makes it tough at home, and made me look at things differently and think of other people a little more. That's why I really didn't mind it when you asked me to help Abby out. I'm kind of used to, I guess, helping people. And I kind of like making people feel better. You know what I mean?"

Kevin was quiet for a moment and then said, "Wow. I'm sorry to hear that, Denise. That's got to be rough."

Denise smiled to bring the conversation into a more upbeat mood. "It is sometimes, but she's getting a little better at doing little things for herself again. So, we're hoping that one day she'll recover and be ok again. You know what I mean?"

Kevin let it drop. "Ok cool! I'm glad to hear that!"

Denise, changing the subject, asked, "So where are we going?"

Kevin looked around. "How 'bout there?" and pointed to some bench tables under a canopy.

"For what?" Denise asked.

"To talk," Kevin said.

"About what?" Denise asked.

Kevin hunched his shoulders and said, "Maybe we can talk about how you just can't chill and walk up on the hill, then sit down and talk. Let's talk about that there! Damn!"

Denise put her head down. "Ok. You're right. It just seems strange seeing you outside of school. It's weird, you know?"

Kevin smiled. "Yeah, I guess it is a little bit. That's ok though, right?"

Denise said, "Yeah it's cool I guess. I just never…"

Kevin interrupted her. "Yeah, I know, right."

They got to the benches at the top of the hill, and the wind flipped the hood of her jacket up onto her head.

Kevin said, "Damn… it's jive cold up here. This may not have been a good idea."

Denise said, "I'm ok if you're ok."

"Cool," Kevin said as they sat down facing each other. Kevin looked at her with a goofy face and said, "So…what the hell ARE we doing?"

Denise laughed. "I know, right man? I don't know, Kevin, I don't know…"

Kevin looked past her. "They say a lot of times in life, what you are looking for is oftentimes right up under your nose.…"

Denise said, "So what is it you think is right up under your nose, Kevin?" Kevin laughed. 'So, we're going to play that game, huh?"

Denise acted coy, "What game is that?"

Kevin sighed and said, "Welp, you've screwed me a couple of times when I jumped out there, but ok, I'll go first....You're cool, really cool. And I think, for real, I've been looking for someone like you for a long time, for a real long time. It's kind of hard to explain...you know what I mean?"

Denise sat quietly for a moment and said, "I guess I've kind of liked you for a long time, but you...were on that 'whore' tip and hooking school all the time, and I'm not about that, you know what I mean? But now you seem to be a lot more focused.... And the thing you did for Abby really made me, I guess, notice you more or think of you as more than just maybe a friend. You've got a good heart, and as much as we pick at each other, that still always comes through. I always knew you were smart, too. You're just so damn stupid sometimes," she said as she smiled and slapped him on his arm.

"Well damn..." Kevin said.

Denise pulled her collar up around her ears as the winds became stronger.

"Come here," Kevin said as he slid himself back on his bench. "What are you doing?" Denise asked as she stood and faced him. "Sit here," as he pointed to a spot between his legs for her to sit.

Denise looked at him suspiciously.

"On the bench, Denise, damn! I'm just trying to block you from the wind. I ain't gonna grab your butt or nothing, come on slim." Kevin said.

Denise stared at him as she slowly sat down between his legs.

"Better?" he asked as she looked at him over her shoulder.

"Unh hunh..." Denise replied, still acting doubtful of his intentions.

"I was that damn bad, huh?" Kevin said laughing.

"Terrible!" she said as she crossed her arms and leaned back into his chest.

Kevin felt the warmth of her body on his and, without even thinking, wrapped his arms around her waist and pulled her in tighter.

Denise half-closed her eyes and crossed her arms over his. "This is nice," she said.

"Yeah, it is." Kevin put his chin on her shoulder, and Denise started to gently rock back and forth. "I don't know where this is going, D, I ain't gonna lie, but I like where it's at right now, that's for damn sure."

Kevin could feel that all-too-familiar warmth rising in his stomach that he came to recognize as 'The fall.'

Denise leaned her head back and smiled. "Me, too."

Kevin said, "All we need is a radio and some Quiet Storm right now, and this would be damned-near perfect."

Denise laughed. "For real! Did you hear it last night? Melvin Lindsay was jamming! Then when he played my favorite, all I could think of was why couldn't I be at a party right now."

Kevin laughed and said, "I know, right! So, what's your favorite?"

"Honey by the Ohio Players," she said. "That song there, wheeww!"

Kevin laughed. "Like that, huh?"

Denise smiled. "Yessss, like that! What's your favorite?" Kevin had to think hard to name a pre-1979 favorite.

"I've got a couple…Cloudy by AWB, This Must Be Heaven by Brainstorm and A Song for You by Rodney Franklin."

Denise sat up and looked back at him, smiling. "Damn boy! Those are some good ones. I figured you'd say the usual Reasons and Always and Forever. You got a little, what you call that, 'Flava,' huh?"

Kevin laughed. "One more…Give Me Time by Minnie. That one hits me. Can you imagine being sick and your one wish is to have more time to love the person you're with? That's what I want. I think that's what everybody wants. To be in love so much that you are less concerned with your own death as you are with the pain that your death will leave your loved one in. That's love right there!"

Denise stopped rocking and sat quietly. "You think you have that in you, to love someone completely like that, forever?" she asked softly.

"Most definitely. But, people that have the capacity to love like that rarely find someone with the same intentions, and are more likely to wind up hurt and alone. Look at the bullet I just dodged with Tiffany. What if I'd went all in and later found out she had another boyfriend? I may fall in love again after that, but never with the same intensity or full commitment. A person learns over time to hold a little of their heart back, just in case the other person isn't real. To me, that's a waste of time. If you're not all in, then why bother? Trust is huge! Steal my money and all my stuff, I can get that back. But to betray a person's trust and purposely break their heart? You kill the trust and the love gets a little weaker each time. I don't want that life, and don't want to be the reason someone else has that life. I don't think anyone does." Kevin said.

Denise frowned and looked at Kevin curiously. "What happened to you man!? Dude, seriously! You were…a ho!"

Kevin laughed. "Damn, shorty! I dump my soul out in front of you, and that's what you got for me? We gonna call that the last time I do that shit right there!"

Denise laughed. "Nah Kevin, but seriously man, you and your boys are out there. What changed? What happened? You're going to class now, talking all philosophical, and killing the grades…what happened?"

Kevin said softly, "I got a new perspective. I kind of see what's important in life. It's not the things you have or how many women you can get. It's deeper than that. People are the real treasures in life."

Denise went quiet again and said softly, "Dude, if you're running game on me, this is a damn good game. I swear, if you are, I'm going to get you seriously busted up, no joke!"

Kevin laughed. "When we get back to your house, I'ma need to see your birth certificate."

Denise smiled. "For what?"

Kevin said, "To see if you were born with balls. You up here threatening me and punching me all the got-damned time!"

Denise looked back at him, "See, there's the stupid Kevin I know right there!"

Kevin laughed, "Whatever slim…so how come you don't have a boyfriend Denise? I never even see you talking to anyone. What's up with that?"

Denise shrugged her shoulders. "I don't know…there are a lot of cute boys I liked and some tried to talk to me. But, they talked about nothing junk like what they have, and what they were going to get, and all that fake crap, like that was supposed to impress me. Every conversation was like that! I mean, ok sometimes, but every time?! There was nothing deep, nothing that involves thought, just superficial stuff all the time! Oh yeah, and sex; lots of talk about sex. I don't care what the subject was, it always led back to them trying to sleep with me. All I knew about them is what they had and were trying to get, and they never took the time to try to know anything about me.

But I'm supposed to get naked and give THIS body to them?! Picture that!"

Kevin laughed. "You're rougher than schoolhouse toilet paper, slim."

Denise laughed. "Nah, seriously! They don't know me from a can of paint, but they want to have sex! That tells me there were probably a lot of other broads they had sex with that they didn't know. These nasty asses ain't sending me to Upshur Clinic, with their dirty selves! Nope!"

Kevin asked, "So you're a virgin?"

Denise paused to weigh her answer. "No, I tried it. I let myself get pressured into it. It didn't feel…right. You know? I didn't love him, didn't even really like him a lot, so it was just… mechanical. I don't know what the big deal about it is, really. But ya'll dudes act like it's water or something. So how many times have you had sex?"

Kevin laughed. "You don't really want to know that, do you?" Denise looked back at him. "Uhhhh, yeah, I do."

Kevin knew from experience that this was bad territory.

"Denise, let's just say more than once. But it doesn't drive me like it used to. Evidence of that is I'm sitting here with you, right?"

Denise smirked. "So, if I said come on let's do it right over there in those bushes right now, you're saying you'd say no? You want me to believe that?"

Kevin laughed. "Nope. I'd light you up over in those bushes right there, right now, I ain't gonna lie to you."

Denise says, "Yeah, that's what I thought."

Kevin says, "But later, I'd be disappointed in you and again be questioning my judgement of people because I'd have thought that you had more respect for yourself and were built out of something better than that. I'd look at you differently. That's the truth."

Denise looked back at him again. "So, you're saying I'd be slutty if I did that, but what does that make you?"

Kevin squeezed her around the waist tighter. "It'd just make me a dude that got some booty from a broad in the bushes."

Kevin cracked up laughing, and Denise acted as if she was trying to break his hold while laughing. "See, that's that crap right there, get off me!"

Kevin straightened up a little. "Nah, seriously though, no dude is going to take an easy girl seriously. Guys damn sure don't want an easy girlfriend, because if he's smart, he knows if it's easy for him, then it's easy for the next man. If you'll go in the bushes with me on the first date, then what the hell would make me think you won't do the same with somebody else just as soon? And especially since I'm a dude who you say is just ALRIGHT, whatever the hell that crap means. I'm alright; ALRIGHT hell. I'm a got-damned beautiful Black man, that's what the hell I am! How you gonna tell me I'm some got-damned 'alright' shit?!"

Denise cracked up laughing, and Kevin acted as if he were pushing her away from him. "What the hell you laughing at? Get up…get off me!"

Denise cried out, laughing, "You stuuupid!"

Denise settled down. "So, Kevin, this is our first date, huh?" Kevin acted as if he were still upset.

"Nope. I'm trying to figure out if I even like you for real at this point."

Denise laughed. "Did I hurt your feelings with alright? Ok, you're cute. How's that, is that better?" she asked as she patted his leg, being condescending.

Kevin shook his head back and forth and said, "It's not…it's not looking good for you slim. It's not."

Denise snapped back. "Don't try to forget that you said I was just ok. What the hell is ok?"

Kevin laughed. "You were ok because you were a got-damned bus driver that kept running my ass over every time I stepped out there with you. That's why you were just ok."

Denise smiled. "So, what am I now?"

Kevin laughed. "You're fishing for compliments. That's what you are now." Denise turned around smiling. "Well, I think I look good."

Kevin said, "Ok."

She put her face close to his and used her sexy voice. "In fact...I think...I look damn good..."

Kevin's face went blank. Denise smiled and turned back around and scooted back on Kevin. She abruptly scooted forward and said, "Whoa." And turned to look back at Kevin, and then at his crotch. She shook her head. "Seriously? You need to fix that man."

Kevin stared at her blankly and said, "Sorry, but I can't do nothing about that. What you should learn from this is, it ain't a game over here."

Denise turned back. "Ok damn, I won't use the sexy voice with you anymore."

Kevin laughed. "Ain't nobody telling you that!" Denise laughed. "You're sick as hell!"

Kevin says, "A little bit, yeah."

Denise smiled. "Well, I guess you obviously find me attractive, despite what your mouth says, huh?"

Kevin thought for a minute. *I find you bad as hell.*

Denise sat up. "Huh?"

Kevin said, "You're bad as hell. You look great, and that's one thing. But your personality puts you way above just good looks. You're bad as hell."

Denise sat quietly. "You ok?" Kevin said.

"Yeah." Denise said quietly.

Kevin looked at her face from the side. "You blushing? Awwwww, 'her' shy for real? Poor baby." He said laughing.

Denise smiled. "Go 'head man…"

Kevin ran with it, whispering in her ear. "When the sun was starting to go down, I was fixated on your eyes. They're beautiful. And the way you look up through your hair at me… and the slight upturn of your top lip…"

Denise interrupted him, "Ok, ok Kevin. You can stop now!" As she bent forward and put her face in her hands.

Kevin laughed. "So, it's agreed. You be cool with the sexy voice in public, and I'll chill with the compliments. Deal?"

Denise turned around and put her hand out to shake his. "That's a bet!" Her face was beet red. Kevin smiled at her.

"Don't look at me!" Denise said as she turned away.

Kevin said, "That's what's up!"

"What?" Denise says.

"You act all tough, but you're not. It's just your way to keep from being taken advantage of. You're a big 'ol softy!"

Denise straightened up. "I'm not a 'big 'ol softy,' as you say. You can cut that."

Kevin sat quietly for a minute, then said, "That's too bad. I'm kind of looking for a girl that's not afraid to show how she feels."

Denise said seriously. "Dudes take advantage of those types of girls." Kevin said, "That's true. There's a chance you can get hurt. But like I said, either you're all in or you're wasting your time. You won't ever get a dollars' worth if all you're giving is 50 cents."

Denise turned to him. "How do you know when to go all in though? And who to go all in with?"

Kevin shook his head. "I guess that's the fun part...you never know. You just gotta have faith I guess, huh?"

Denise turned back around. "Having faith in you dudes is real hard to do."

Kevin said, "I hear you. I guess the best thing to do is walk slow and listen more than you talk. One thing for sure is you can't make a person be what or who you want them to be. Accept their flaws or move on. And everyone has flaws."

Denise sat quietly for a second and asked, "So, what's your flaw?"

Kevin smiled and said in her ear, "I'm cursed with being beautiful."

Denise laughed. "Let me find out you're conceited!"

Kevin laughed. "Nah, I'm jiving. I just like me again. A little while ago I didn't. It's cool. I see things differently than I did before. Life is good when you're doing the right thing. I didn't always do the right thing, or appreciate what I had."

Denise says, "I never knew you didn't like yourself. Never knew you had a serious side either. All you ever did was play in class and joke."

Kevin says, "And all you did was joke and swing that weak-assed right hook at me all the time. I should have known back then, though."

Denise says, "Known what?"

Kevin says, "Girls that hit you like that all the time like you. It's their way of getting your attention."

Denise laughed. "Boy please! Ain't nobody like your skinny butt back then!" Kevin says, "Back then, huh?"

Denise smiled, slowly turned her head toward him, and then slowly looked back away.

Kevin said, "Be careful."

Denise asked, "Why?"

Kevin replied, "I'm awesome!"

Denise laughed. "I'm awesome too, though. YOU'D better be careful!"

Kevin hugged her tighter around her waist and says, "Yup, I'll try."

Denise crossed her hands over his again and leaned back and says, "Don't try too hard though….Oh my God, what time is it?" she said frantically.

Kevin pushed back his sleeve. "It's…7:47, why?"

Denise said, "We've got to get back. Abby said she needed to call me about something important at 8:00. It sounded serious."

Kevin helped her to her feet. "Ok. Let's roll." Kevin walked her to her door. "I'll see you tomorrow, Kev," Denise said.

"Kev, huh? Awwwww, it's sweet little nickname time, huh?"

Denise straightened her face and said, "Remember when I said you were really stupid sometimes? Yeah, like that right there."

Kevin laughed as he hugged her. "My bad….I'll see you tomorrow, honey bunny."

Denise pushed him off, laughing. "Bye BOY! Stupid self!"

Kevin backed down the stairs. "Alright Dee, I'll see you tomorrow."

Denise smiled. "Dee, huh?"

Kevin kept walking and without looking back said, "That's right!"

Denise walked into the house smiling, and was greeted by her mother's stare in the kitchen.

"Oh Oh…" Her mom said.

"Mom, it's not even like that," Denise said as she bound up the stairs. "Yeah ok young lady, ok…" her mom responded.

Denise came in homeroom late, arriving after Kevin for a change.

She sat behind him and Kevin said sarcastically, "Just show up any time you want to…like that's alright and shit huh?"

Denise sat and didn't say anything. Kevin turned around and looked at her, "You alright?" he asked.

She kept the same blank face, and Kevin said, "It's me?"

She said, "Nah, something else, it's ok."

Kevin got that "'Bout to fight" feeling in his stomach and asked, "Abby?" Denise sat quietly for a minute and then said, "I can't talk about it…"

Kevin figured that Abby probably confessed to Denise what was going on in her house with her father.

Kevin asked, "Are YOU ok?"

Denise said, "I'm alright, seriously…just jive messed up a little bit, you know…."

Kevin put his hand over hers. "I know, but if you need to talk…"

Denise looked at his hand and looked up in his eyes. "I know, thanks."

Kevin turned around in his seat. A few minutes later, he felt Denise's hand straightening out the back of his shirt collar into his sweater. He turned around and she just smiled at him. It was a different kind of smile, though. Kevin smiled back, turned around and thought to himself, *Damn...Shorty cool as hell.* Kevin straightened his face when HE noticed he was smiling to himself. Just then, there was a tap on the window of the back door. Kevin looked over and saw that it was James, waving to him to come out of the classroom. Kevin looked at James, and then Denise, and then back at James. Kevin shook his head no and then pulled his hand across his neck to signal, *'That's dead.'* James gave him a disappointed look and then walked away. Kevin turned back in his chair and could feel Denise giving him a pat on his back.

Kevin said, "So I'm a dog now?"

Denise said, "I hope not."

Kevin whipped around in his chair and sees that she's smiling that smile again.

He smiled back, turns around and said, "Don't play with me Shorty, It ain't a game over here."

He could hear Denise snicker, and then she said, "Again, I hope not."

Kevin laughed and leaned back in his chair and said loudly, "FLAVA!!!"

Denise laughed out loud and, from the front of the class, Mr. Scott yelled, "Be quiet back there!"

Kevin turned and said, "Meet me on the hill at lunch."

Denise quietly said, "Ok".

Next Class: Black History, Mr. Colbert

Kevin got to the class to find Mr. Colbert sitting at his desk reading the paper.

After everyone was seated and without looking up, he said, "Assignment is on the board, and study Chapter 5 for Thursday's Test." He then turned the page of the newspaper he was reading.

Kevin said loud enough for Mr. Colbert to hear him, "I wonder what new Black subject we'll read about today, ahhhh, my main man from 3rd grade, Frederick Douglas!"

Some of the students laughed, causing Mr. Colbert to look over his paper and ask, "Is there something amusing about today's assignment that I missed?"

Kevin says, "No sir. There's nothing funny at all about this class."

Mr. Colbert pushed his paper down and looked at Kevin. "Is there something you want to say, Mr. Allen?"

Kevin smiled. "No sir. I'll just read here on how we were slaves, or trying not to be slaves, or fighting for our civil rights, or… never mind. There's nothing in this book about who we were before slavery. We're all just some aliens that fell to Earth, I guess. As slaves"

Mr. Colbert sat up. "Very funny, Kevin. Maybe you'd like to enlighten the class with some of your vast knowledge of Black History."

Kevin sat up. "Seriously?"

Mr. Colbert smiled. "Of course, I'm dying to learn something from a student who has cut my class so much I've stopped calling their name in roll call. You were obviously doing self-study down at the library, isn't that right?" he said sarcastically.

Kevin smiled and held up the book. "This book, and books like it, are garbage. Most of the books provided to us by this school system are garbage. This book tells nothing about Africa or how our ancestors were on just about every continent, including this one, BEFORE Columbus who, by the way, was not some great pioneer that discovered America but was more of a lackluster captain of a lost ship. But, that's what you can do when you write your own history, and this is what you get when you let someone else write your story," he said as he plopped the book back down on his desk.

The class, who had been staring at Kevin as he spoke, turned their attention back to the teacher.

Mr. Colbert smiled. "So, Mr. Allen, if I give you the Thursday test right now, do you think you'll pass it? I mean since, as you say, this is something you've been repeatedly studying since the 3rd grade…"

Kevin laughed. "If I study that thing for 5 minutes, seriously, I don't see me getting any less than a B on your test. It's garbage!"

Mr. Colbert looked at Kevin sternly for a long moment, with his face red as a beet, nodded his head, and then smiled. "Ok Mr. Allen (he said as he rounded his desk, reached into the drawer and pulled out a folder), you're on! I'll give you 10 minutes to study, but here's the catch. Whatever grade you get on the test will be your grade for this quarter. That way you can put your money where your mouth is," he said as he smacked the folder onto the desk.

Kevin laughed and said, "Garbage..." as he stared back into Mr. Colbert's eyes, looking unphased.

"Ok.... You've got 10 minutes, starting now, to study Chapter 5. Get started!"

Before Kevin flipped the book open, he looked up and addressed the class. "Ya'll think I hooked this class because I'm dumb, or the work was too hard, huh? I hooked this class because this crap is boring! Who, What, When, Where, and Why, folks... that's all you need to memorize."

Kevin turned to Chapter 5 and started reading. Most of the class had their heads down, pretending that they were studying, but were watching him as he flipped through the pages.

Six minutes later, Kevin closed his eyes, looked like he was talking to himself for a minute, and then said, "I'm ready."

Mr. Colbert walked to the back of the class and handed Kevin the test as he removed Kevin's book from his desk and walked back to the front of the class. "You may begin at any time you wish, Mr. Allen."

Kevin flipped open the folder and said, "Multiple choice! Awwwww man!" he said, smiling, as he began to write his answers on a separate piece of paper. There were 15 questions on the test. After about 4 minutes, Kevin closed the folder and stood. He had the folder in one hand, and his test in the other. As he walked toward the front of the class, he caught the eye of Cynthia Boone as she tried to 'mean mug' him. He looked at her with the kind of smirk that he'd hoped relayed the thought, 'garbage.'

Kevin placed the folder on Mr. Colbert's desk, but before he gave him his test, he asked, "How about just one more stipulation?" and smiled.

Mr. Colbert lit up. "This should be interesting, go on…"

Kevin said, "If I get a B or better, I get to teach the class for 15 minutes once a week, Deal?"

Mr. Colbert says, "If the subject person is a Black American, I don't see why not."

Kevin handed the teacher his paper and, as he was walking back to his seat, his eyes made contact with Tiffany Brown. She looked at him with a sad face and mouthed the words, "I'm sorry."

Kevin shrugged his shoulders at her and sat down. He noticed she was sitting away from Cynthia Boone. *Good*, he thought to himself. *Maybe she finally got some sense and left that bum-sauce broad alone.*

Kevin looked up to see Mr. Colbert, red pen poised, grading his paper. He flipped the first page over and hadn't marked on it. Kevin was confident in all his answers except one.

Mr. Colbert finished the last page and turned the first one back over. He wrote something on the first page, and shook his head side-to-side, grinning.

Kevin looked around the class, as the whole class was either looking at him or looking at the teacher.

Mr. Colbert looked at Kevin and said, "You'll have to run your subject by me first for approval." Someone in the class yelled "Daaaamn Shorty!!!" and everyone started laughing.

QUIET!" Mr. Colbert said as he slammed a book on the desk.

Everyone settled down.

"Congratulations on your A for this quarter, Mr. Allen," as he smiled at Kevin with a sarcastic face that really didn't convey a happy feeling.

Bruce jumped out of his seat, gave Kevin hard 'dap' handshake, and shouted "Chess Team, BOY!!", and then punched himself across his chest.

Kevin laughed and said, "Ok, the Chess Team's doing that now, huh?" Bruce was standing like he just tackled somebody. "That's right!"

Kevin caught Tiffany looking over at Cynthia and 'mean-mugging' her. Cynthia looked at her and rolled her eyes back forward. At that moment, Kevin felt a little sorry for Tiffany, but just a little.

Kevin grabbed two strawberry Nehi sodas and two packs of Krispy Kreme jelly doughnuts, and sat on a bench in the park on the hill waiting for Denise.

As he was waiting, Bobby drove by, slowed and yelled, "What up Kev! You good?"

Kevin yelled back, "Yeah, I'm Good! Just waiting on my girl to get here!"

Kevin thought to himself, *My boy Bobby, we were cool as hell until I started going out with his sister. Note to self, never date your buddy's sister. Even though she was...NAH...don't date her.*

Kevin could only guess that his time out with his thoughts lasted a little longer than he anticipated, because right then, Bobby points and says, "Oh ok, one of them?"

Kevin looked around and saw Denise and Abby standing behind him. Kevin looked back at Bobby with his eyes big and his mouth open, and Bobby put a stupid smirk on his face, acted as if he was adjusting his rear-view mirror, looked forward, and drove off laughing with his patented "BWAAAAHHHHH!!!" laugh.

Kevin dropped his head and said, "Gaaaaaadamn!"

Abby started laughing and doing some stupid dance, saying, "I knew it! I knew it!"

Kevin and Denise just looked at Abby with stone faces, and then Denise said, "Hey Abby, I need to talk to Kevin for a second, could you give me a minute?"

Abby walks away still all giddy. "I told you! I knew it!"

Denise turned back to Kevin trying to hold in her smile. "Soooo...I'm your girl, huh? Like your buddy, or your girl-girl?" she asked.

Kevin thought to himself, *Hell with it!*, leaned back on his elbows, and without looking at her, said, "My girl-girl."

Denise laughed. "So, you aren't even going to ask me, huh?" she said, with her hands on her hips. "You gonna just tell me, huh?!"

Kevin looked over at her. "I just told you!"

Denise stepped back, acting as if she were offended. "That's some cocky shit, man!"

Kevin said, "Nope, that's confidence. You like that shit!" and laughed.

Denise laughed, shook her head, and then said, "Nah, nah you gotta ask me if I want to be your girl!"

Kevin turned around and looked at her as if he were tired, sighed loudly, stood up, walked directly in front of her, hiked up his right pant leg, and as he began to bend down on one knee,

Denise punched him, laughed, and said, "Boy you'd better not embarrass me out here like that!"

He came up and she gave him a hug and a quick kiss on the lips.

Kevin said, "We gotta work on that kissing thing. I'll give up on some things, but not that!"

Denise smiled that smile, used her sexy voice, and said, "Oh, you mean like this…" With their eyes closed and a park full of people, all they could hear was Abby as she kept yelling in the distance, "YES!!! YES!!! YES!!!"

They broke their kiss, and Kevin quickly sat down on the bench. "What's wrong with you?" Denise asked with concern.

"Nothing," Kevin replied. "Want a soda?"

Denise picked up his chin in her hand and looked at him with concern. "What's wrong with you, Kevin?"

Kevin put his head down, then looked her back in her eyes, and said with a serious voice, "You broke it again. It's harder than got-damned ox ankles. You want some soda?"

Denise looked at him, slowly realized what he said, and busted out laughing, leaning onto the bench seat and practically crying.

Kevin popped the top on his soda, took a swig, and looked over at her as she laughed and said, "That's alright shorty, you gonna appreciate this one day, I guarantee you that," which only made Denise laugh even harder.

Abby ran up the hill to them saying, "What…WHAT?"

Kevin looked at her calmly and said, "Nothing. You want got-damned Denise's soda?" as he held it up to Abby, which made Denise laugh even more.

Abby took the soda, started drinking it, and said, "These too?" as she pointed at the pack of doughnuts.

"Hell yeah!" Kevin said.

As he turned to laugh, Kevin looked across the street and saw two girls walking. One was his future or past? Ex-wife. He looked to his right and saw the crap game that he won that day so many years ago, when he was hooking school. Damn, today is that day! Right about now he remembers standing up, passing the dice, and hollering at the two girls across the street to stop.

That's when he got his ex-wife's number. That's the day…THIS IS THE DAY!

Kevin looked over at Denise getting herself together and thought to himself, *Left turn like a son of a bitch!* He took another swig of his soda as he watched his future ex-wife round the corner. *Déjà vu my ass*, he said to himself as he smiled.

"Denise, I've got a game today, you coming?" Kevin asked. "Uhhhh, sit there and watch you play Chess? I'm going to pass on that one but good luck!" She said with heavy sarcasm.

Kevin gave her a blank look and said, "Nope. I'm not going to call you a name because we go together now. Tennis Denise. Tennis. Would you like to come to my Tennis match?"

"Oh Tennis! Yeah ok. Who are we playing?"

Kevin shook his head as if in disbelief and said, "Spingarn I think. At home after school."

Denise said, "Yeah ok, Abby you want to see the game before we go to the library?"

"No, you two go ahead, I'll just meet you at the Library when it's over so that you two can get some alone time." She said smiling.

Kevin and Denise just looked at each other and shook their heads.

Kevin was down 0-6 when the two players switched sides. He walked over to the bench Denise was sitting on and grabbed his towel to wipe his face. Denise looked at him questioningly and said, "What is this?"

Kevin wiped his face and threw the towel back onto the bench. "What is what?" he asked.

"This isn't how I've seen you play Tennis when you're hitting with your boys Austin and David. WHAT IS THIS!" She asked again.

Kevin said, "Yeah that's how we hit when we're just jiving around. This is a match. I'm trying to keep the ball in play."

Denise crossed her arms and said, "Ok. Go ahead and keep dinking the ball over the net so he can keep smashing it past you then. Looks like your way is working so far.", and turned her head away from him.

Kevin stared at her for a moment. "You've got a point."

Denise without looking back at him said, "Damn right I got a point." She then looked back at him and said, "Hey Kev, if you lose, lose because you lost, not because you just let somebody beat you. I'm just saying man…"

Kevin walked over to his side, gathered up two tennis balls and said to her, "You're right!".

His first serve was out. His competitor walked up closer for his second serve that Kevin had been just, as Denise said, *dinking* over the net.

Kevin hit his second serve just as hard as he did the first. ACE!

Denise smiled and gave Kevin her, "I Told you so" look.

Kevin went on to win the match 10-6.

After the match, Denise walked up to him with a fake serious look on her face and said, "If you're going to be my boyfriend, you better not ever let me catch you half doing something again! You got that!" As she grabbed his shirt.

"Yes Ma'am!" Kevin said acting as if he was scared.

She let him go laughing and Kevin said, "Me and you together! WHAT! Isn't no stopping us shorty!" And she gave him a high five.

Kevin said, "Nah. We're about to start something new! Ball your fist up. Denise said, "Like this?"

"Yeah, now hit my fist." He said.

She did it and said, "Like that?"

Kevin said, "Yeah. That's our high five from now on. Pound it!"

Denise laughed. "You're always doing some new crap man..."

Kevin laughed. "That's because we're Kevin and Denise! We're about to teach this whole school what a relationship is supposed to look like!" Kevin said.

"Oh really..." Denise said in her sexy voice. Kevin stopped laughing immediately. "Go 'head with that shorty. I got these little Tennis shorts on man..." Denise put her hand over her mouth laughing. "I'm sorry. I didn't mean to..."

Kevin interrupted her. "Yeah, yeah go 'head with that shit slim..."

They both laughed.

Kevin turned to Denise. "Hey, let's celebrate and go out this weekend."

Denise sighed, "Abby and I are supposed to go to the movies, though." Kevin said, "Cool, we'll go to the movies, then."

"I said I'm going with Abby," Denise said.

Kevin said, "I'll get my boy to come with us."

Denise grabbed Kevin's arm. "Your boy who? Not one of the Gray brothers, I hope!"

Kevin said, "Nah, nah, my boy Bobby."

Denise asked, "Bobby with the car? Ok, cool!"

Kevin laughed, "Then it's a date, then!"

Kevin got home and called Bobby. "Hey Bobby, keep the weekend open, man."

Bobby answered, "Who's throwing the party?"

"Nah man, I need you to hit this date with me and Denise this Friday. I got a girl for you," Kevin said.

"Who, shorty? I'm not going to wing man for you if you got me set up with some woolly-looking broad, the hell with that!" replied Bobby.

Kevin laughed. "I wouldn't do you like that man. It's Abby, the girl you saw us with up on the hill."

Bobby's voice got animated. "Oh, hell yeah! Little shorty was bad! That's a bet, man. Good looking out; I was going to ask you about her anyway. DAMN! Good looking out, man!"

Kevin laughed. "Alright man, bet then. Be ready around 4-4:30. Cool? Bobby laughed and said, "Man I'll be at your house at 3!"

Kevin said, "Alright man, cool. Later."

Bobby replied, "Later," and hung up.

Kevin then called Denise. Trey answered the phone.

"Denise, it's Keeeeevinnnnn," he said.

Kevin could hear Denise approach the phone. "Boy, you'd better stop playing with me," she said as she laughed.

Kevin could hear her wrestling with Trey and him laughing. "Go downstairs, Trey!"

Trey was making kissing sounds as he was leaving her room.

"And close my door!" Denise told Trey.

Kevin could hear the door close, and Trey laughing in the distance.

"Little brothers, ugggggghhhhh," Denise said.

Kevin laughed. "I've got a little sister, Dee. I know all about the struggle." They both laughed.

"So, what's up?" Denise asked.

"I just talked to Bobby, and it's a go for Friday. We can swing by and pick you up first, and then go get Abby, cool?"

Denise thought about it for a second. "You can pick us both up from my house. By the time we get back, her father should be gone to work and Bobby can drop her off then. I'm going to get her to come straight to my house after school, so she won't have to deal with her Pop's."

Kevin said, "It's like that over there?"

"Yeah, it's like that," Denise said.

"Aye, let's get something to eat before we go to the movies. How 'bout you pick the movie, and I pick the food?" Kevin suggested.

"Ok, Mr. Big Money," Denise said as she laughed.

"Don't worry, I got y'all," Kevin replied.

"Oh, your pockets are like that, huh?" said Denise.

"You ain't noticed me leaning when I'm sitting down? My wallet's fat like a Bible, girl! Nah, just jiving. I'm thinking Shakey's pizza, don't get all excited," Kevin said as he laughed.

Denise laughed. "Ohhhhh, I thought for a second you were going to try to impress me with your money like those other bamas I told you about."

Kevin laughed. "Nah shorty, I'm broke. But I got a hustle, so I don't plan on being broke for long."

"What hustle?" Denise asked seriously.

"I'm doing signs now. What did you think I meant, selling weed or something?" Kevin asked.

"I'm just checking. You know how I feel about drugs. This would have been our last call. Date cancelled. No more boyfriend/ girlfriend. Nothing," she said.

"That's what's up! Good, because I can't stand a drug dealer. They destroy people, and if I ever find out you try some, I'm busting you straight in the mouth. And I don't hit girls," Kevin said.

"And if I find out you try it, I'm busting you in your mouth, too!" Denise said.

Kevin laughed. "Say you'll stab me or something shorty. That weak-assed hook you got ain't exactly a deterrent."

Denise laughed. "Yeah ok. But I'm glad were on the same page with that. Seriously though, you need me to bring some money to help out?"

"Nah Dee, I got us! You're my girl, right? I got us!" Kevin said.

"Well, I'm bringing something anyways. My father always told me to never go anywhere with anybody and not be able to get back by yourself if you have to," Denise said.

Kevin laughed. "What am I? Some damned serial killer that's going to 'Kirk' out on you on the date or something?"

"You never know man. Plus, I'm just taking your advice. I'm taking it slow, listening, and watching."

Kevin laughed. "You were doing all of that before we even went together. You tree-boxed the hell out of me at the Wilson game!...'I saw you flirting with that cheerleader,'" he said, mocking her voice.

Denise laughed. "Boy, whatever! What the hell is tree-boxing? You keep coming up with these country-assed words and sayings, I swear!"

"Tree-boxing means to spy on someone from a distance, like you were doing, tree-boxing." Kevin said.

"Wasn't nobody spying on your skinny butt! I just saw you down there dancing with her," Denise said.

"Yeah, then you saw her standing there after the game waiting for me to come over and talk to her. You were spying. You were jealous. You liked me," Kevin said as he laughed.

Denise paused for a second. "Ok. I did. I thought your dumb butt was about to get yourself into another Tiffany situation."

"Oh, ok. It wasn't because you liked me, it was because you were just worried about your friend getting hurt. That's what you're telling me then, right? Not because you liked me; got it!" Kevin said.

"So, you want me to step out there, huh?" Denise said as she sighed.

"I figure it's your turn, don't you? Damn if you haven't squished me under some bus tires every time I tell you something. A dollar for a dollar's worth, slim," Kevin said.

"Kevin, I like you. I've liked you for a long time, ok?" Denise said as fast as she could.

"Seriously? It's that hard for you to tell somebody how you feel? Ok, it's cool. Baby steps, I guess," Kevin said as he laughed. "Was that so hard?"

"Kevin, you know where we come from. We've been joking each other hard back and forth since the 7th grade man. So yeah, for me to tell you that I like you is that hard, ok. Just let me work this out. Be patient, ok?" Denise said.

"Take all the time you need, Dee. I'm not going anywhere unless you tell me to. I'm cool, slim," Kevin said.

"Man, you got me up in here starting to sweat and carrying on, pressing me out. Jeez!" Denise said.

"I'm pressing you out? Ok," Kevin said.

"I didn't mean it like that; I'm just saying, man," Denise said.

"And I'm just listening," Kevin replied.

"Come on Kevin, seriously, don't be like that." Denise said.

"I'm all about the baby steps, Denise, don't get me wrong. But my intent is to eventually be all in with you. When you show me that you're not going in that direction, I start to throttle back, too. Neither one of us wants to get busted in the chest, right? So, we jump at the same time or we don't jump.

That's how I see it," Kevin said.

Denise sighed. "You're right. I'm sorry. It's just that….. never mind. You're right, you're right...I got you."

Kevin thought to himself, *She said you're right and I'm sorry. Never in the history of ever has any woman he'd messed with in his other life said those words to him. This one here. This one here might be the one!*

"It's cool, Dee. And while we're about being pressed out, I'm not going to be pressing you out about sex. When that time comes, it will be because you're ready and want to do it. So, you won't have to worry about me pressing you out about that, ok?" Kevin said.

Denise laughed. "Now I KNOW some aliens must have snatched the real Kevin up and left a clone!"

Kevin laughed. "Ok shorty. I guess I can show you better than I can tell you." Denise whispered into the phone, "Even if I used my sexy voice?"

Kevin sat quietly for a second and then replied, "You need to stop playing, slim. It ain't a game over here, I'm trying to tell you."

Denise laughed and said, "Yeah ok, when I'm ready. And WHEN I'm ready, you'd better be about it, or I'm going to joke the hell out of you, I swear!"

"WHEN you're ready, you'd better drink a lot of fluids before we get started, because I guarantee you're going to lose a lot! How 'bout that!" Kevin said.

Denise laughed. "Yeah, we'll see!"

"Nah, YOU'LL see got-dammit! YOU'LL SEE!" Kevin said.

Denise laughed and said, "Hey, I gotta get off this phone and get my stuff ready for tomorrow. Bye, Kev."

"Bye, babes. I'll see you tomorrow. Good night." Kevin hung up the phone.

Shorty is alright! he thought to himself as he smiled. *Yup! Shorty is alright!*

Kevin walked into the next room, and there sat David at the table doing his homework. "'Bout time," David said, not looking up.

"Bout time what?" Kevin replied.

"Bout time you learned how to talk to girls and not be all, give me some booty, give me some booty, what about some booty. Kev, you were terrible, man!" David said.

Kevin laughed. "I was that bad, huh man?"

"TERRIBLE!" David replied.

"Yeah, I guess I was, damn," Kevin said.

David looked up at Kevin. "Awwwww hell, shorty got a hook in your mouth, huh man? I ain't gonna even joke you. That's what's up, Kev," David said as he smiled at him.

David laughed. "Go 'head man! Yeah, Denise jive got me. She's cool as hell."

"Yeah well, don't mess it up being Kevin. I heard your speech in there, but I know you. So, don't mess it up," David said.

"Nah, D. That's old Kevin, you know. This is the new and improved Kevin 2.0. Trust me, I know how hard it is to find a good one. I'm not messing this up."

"Two point what? Man, you're talking Kevinese again. Half the time I don't know what the hell you're talking about man, I swear," David said.

"I'm from the future!" Kevin said waving his hands up and down with his eyes bulging as he backed out of the room.

David smirked. "There's the one I know, stupid-acting Kevin. Yup, I know that guy," David said as he watched his brother leave.

"Aye, this look alright?" Bobby said as he came up the steps to Kevin's house.

"Nah man, I'm 'bout to put on a suit. Hurry up and change, it's a date man," Kevin said in a serious tone.

Bobby stopped on the steps and asked, "Seriously?"

Kevin said, "Nah, but that's what you get for asking another dude 'how do I look'."

Bobby said, "Come on man, we boys. Seriously, is this ok?" as he motioned to his clothing.

"I wouldn't give a damn if you were wearing a glitter gold Speedo and an orange tie man! I'm doing my thing, and you do your thing," Kevin said.

Bobby just stood there staring at Kevin

Kevin said, "Shit, yeah, man, that looks ok. Ok?"

Bobby smiled and climbed the stairs up to the porch. "My man! You ready?" "In a little bit, come on in."

Bobby came inside and saw Jean in the kitchen. "Hey Jean," he yelled. "Hey Bobby! Where y'all going all dressed up?" Jean asked.

"Me and Kevin 'bout to go out on this date," Bobby said.

Jean looked at Kevin side-eyed and said, "I knew it..." and turned back away.

Kevin chimed in, "We're going with my girl Denise and a girl named Abby. Don't even play like that, Jean!"

Bobby started laughing. "Ahhhhhggghhhhhh! She trying to say you're gay!" and started laughing with Jean.

Kevin said, "She's trying to say you're gay, too, if we were going out on a date, man."

Bobby straightened up and stopped laughing. "Yeah Jean, don't even play like that."

Jean laughed and started up the stairs.

Bobby said, "Glad I ain't got a little sister, damn man."

Kevin laughed. "Nah man, that's my heart right there."

Jean had looked out for Kevin more times than he could count in his other life. She showed her love for him a million times. *Gotta hit her with a couple of dollars or buy her some skates or something,* he thought to himself.

"Aye so man, what's up with Abby? She cool?" Bobby asked.

"Yeah, she's cool. She's got some problems at home, but she's cool. Just take it easy with her, man. She's a good girl," Kevin said.

"Good girl? Virgin?" Bobby asked.

"Maybe. You cool with that?" Kevin asked.

"Man, after dealing with all these damn hookers out here, damn right I'm cool with that!" Bobby said.

"Cool. Let me throw my stuff on, and I'll call and tell Dee we're on our way." Kevin said.

"Dee, huh? I hear you Kev. That's what's up, man. Hope my little shorty turns into Ab, you know what I'm saying?" Bobby said.

Kevin smiled. "Yessir!"

After the movies, Bobby dropped Kevin and Denise off first, and said he'd be back after he took Abby home.

"Take your time!" Kevin yelled at Bobby. "Oh, I will!" Bobby yelled back.

Abby smiled back at Denise from the front seat, and gave a long, "Byyyyyyeeeeee," as they left.

Denise said, "Bobby's cool. That was a good idea, and don't tell him I told you. But Abby told me, when ya'll were buying tickets, that she really likes him."

Kevin said, "We'll don't tell her I told you, but when we were buying tickets, Bobby told me that he really likes her."

They both looked at each other laughing and Denise said, "So, I guess we'll tell them tomorrow then!"

Kevin said, "Yeah, right!"

Denise walked up to Kevin, grabbed him around his side, and said, "Well Mr. Allen, I had a really nice time."

Kevin pulled Denise in close. "Did you...did you..." and kissed her.

The porch light came on, and they heard Denise's mother yell, "Denise, is that you?"

Denise yelled back, "Yeah Mom, I'm coming in now."

Kevin pulled back from her and said, "You should probably start wearing matching underwear sets, something nice."

Denise looked at him puzzled as he walked down the steps. "Why do you say that?" she asked.

Kevin turned back to her, looked at her pelvic area, and said, "It's just a matter of time now before you ask me if we can..." and turned back toward the sidewalk.

Denise picked up the newspaper off the porch and threw it at him as he walked toward the street. Kevin heard the paper land and said, "Confidence baby! You love it! Your man got that FLAVA!"

Denise laughed and said, "You're stupid!" and walked into the house and started up the stairs.

Denise's mother asked, "How was the date?"

Denise said through a big smile, "It was ok."

Her mother laughed, "Looks like it was better than ok. Do I need to have that talk with you?"

Denise snapped serious. "No Ma, NO! I don't need to have 'the talk.' We had fun. That's all! Ok?"

Denise mother laughed. "Ok Denise. Did you bring your father's newspaper in?"

Denise slumped her shoulders and headed out the door. She bent down to pick up the paper and saw Kevin standing by the corner trying to light his cigarette.

"That's what you get!" she yelled at him.

Kevin looked up. "Denise, Denise...you got a light or some matches?" Denise said, "They're in the house."

Kevin stood silently looking at her as if to say, "Could you get them?"

Denise sighed and said, "Wait boy!" then went back in the house and past her mother to get some matches from the junk drawer in the kitchen.

"What's wrong?" Denise's mother asked.

Denise held up the matches and said, "Kevin."

"Ok, hurry back inside, though," her mother said.

Denise walked up to Kevin with the matches. "Here!" acting annoyed.

Kevin took the matches, lit his cigarette and then put the book of matches in his pocket.

"So, you're just going to 'rough the matches off' like that, huh man?" Denise asked with her arms folded.

Kevin pulled the matches back out. "My fault. It looked like y'all were doing good financially. I didn't know a book of matches would break the monthly budget. Here," as he extended his hand to give her back the matches.

"Keep 'em!" she said as she turned back toward the house.

Kevin watched her take a few steps away and said, "I might love you." Denise stopped and turned, smiling. "Yeah, right!"

She then looked at Kevin's face with a serious expression. "Don't play like that," she said.

Kevin turned to look back up the street for Bobby's car.

"KEVIN!" Denise said in a serious tone.

Kevin looked back toward her and said, "That's how I'm feeling. I didn't say it for a reaction or answer from you. I just want you to know how I'm feeling.

And like we talked about on that hill, I just want you to know where I'm at, Ok? So, at any time, let me know if you're not feeling me, so I can stop myself from going all in. Ok?"

Denise nodded her head up and down and slowly turned to walk back toward her house. She started up the stairs to the house, stopped on the steps, and said just loud enough for Kevin to hear, "I might love you, too Kev."

Kevin turned in time to see her entering her house and closing the door. He stared at the door. Thinking about all the bad relationships he'd been in and all the times he'd been screwed over, for an instant, he felt fear in his stomach. But just as suddenly, he believed that he could trust her.

Completely. And he allowed himself to go with the flow. With Denise, he decided, he could go all in.

Denise entered the house and halfway up the stairs to the second floor, she stopped, looked into the kitchen at her mom, then sat on the steps and put her head in her hands.

Her mom saw her and said quietly, "Go in the den and wait for me, I'll be in as soon as I put the food away."

Denise stood and walked quietly to the den and sat on the couch.

Bobby pulled up finally and as soon as Kevin got in the car Bobby grabbed Kevin's jacket and started shaking him back and forth saying, "GOOD LOOKING OUT MAN! GOT DAMN! GOOD LOOKING OUT!"

Kevin laughed and pried Bobby's hand from him. "Damn man come on! The hell did she do to you?"

Bobby, still excited said, "Shorty is cool as shit man! And that kiss…DAMN! Yeah. I'll wait for that one! If she kisses like that I know the sex is going to be off the got damn chain!"

Kevin laughed at him. "Got damn shame…girl got you whipped off a damn kiss. You embarrassed me out there pimpin'." Bobby laughed.

"Say what you want. Call me what you want. Don't care! That's going to be my wife one day watch! Shorty is like that! She got light brown eyes with like, a green ring around them. You see 'em?"

Kevin laughed. "Nah man. Too busy looking at Denise."

'Shorty what's that thing you say…that's my flavor right there!' Bobby said. Kevin looked over at Bobby and said, "Soooo… she's badder than Allison?"

Bobby looked back at Kevin with a serious face and said, "Who?" And then burst out laughing and leaning on him as only Bobby does.

As soon as Kevin came through his front door Jean says to him, "Kevin that girl called…Denise. Said you should call her when you get in. Who would want to talk to you? Uggggghhhhh…"

Kevin's mother saw the exchange and turned chuckling to herself into the kitchen.

"That's funny Ma? Ok. That's how ya'll do me huh?" He said in a laughing tone.

She didn't answer.

Kevin yelled as he walked up the steps toward his room, "All this love in this house! I hardly know what to do with myself!"

As soon as he entered the room David said, "Hey man, Denise called. You should call her back. It sounded important."

Kevin's heart started beating as he started imagining the worst. *"Is she alright? Is she in trouble?"* He grabbed the phone and called her. "Hello?" she said.

"Hey! It's me. Everything alright?" Kevin said excitedly.

Denise hesitated for a moment. "Yeah Kev. Everything's alright...look man...don't play with me...ok?"

Kevin said, "What...what are you talking about Denise?"

"It's...that thing we talked about...on the hill that day..." She said.

"What thing?" he asked.

"You know, about going all in...I'm saying...ok."

Kevin paused for a while and said, "Ok? Like ok you're willing to go all in?" Denise said quietly, "Yeah, I guess...I mean yeah."

Kevin laughed.

"WHAT'S SO DAMN FUNNY!" Denise asked angrily.

Kevin said, "Man you all late! Hell, I decided I was going to go all in at the Tennis match! Go 'head somewhere with your late assed feelings!"

Denise burst out laughing and said, "YOU STUPID!"

Kevin said, "Oh I'm stupid. At least I know when I'm in love! Your dumb ass walking around saying I like him, a lot a lot, a whole lot, a really lot!"

Denise laughed and said, "So you love me?"

Kevin said, "First thing I think about when I wake up. Last thing I think about when I go to sleep. Whenever I think about you I smile and when I think about kissing you I get this crazy feeling in my stomach soooo..." Denise interrupted him and said, "You just described everything I'm going through damn!"

Kevin laughed and said, "I warned you that I was awesome!"

Denise laughed and said, "That's alright, you got got too slim!"

Kevin said, "True dat, true dat, so we're in huh?"

Denise says, "Looks like it, doesn't it?"

"All in?" Kevin asked.

"Ok...what does *All In* mean to you Kevin?" Denise said.

Kevin sighed, "It means if I say I'm out with my boys, you won't act suspicious, it means if you see me talking to another female, you know we're just talking and I'm not trying to crack on her. It means you should know in your heart and mind that I've got your best interest and feelings in mind always. You represent me, I represent you. It means we are now partners and the things we do, we do for us and not just as individuals anymore. It means that you have to trust me completely."

The phone was silent on the other end for what seemed like minutes. Denise finally said, "Well damn! That's like being married, isn't it?"

Kevin laughed and said, "Oh yeah, it also means that you're going into this with that being your goal. For us to one day be married."

"You're serious?' Denise said.

"Dead serious. Why start something that you don't plan on finishing?" Kevin said.

The phone went silent again.

"You ok over there Mrs. Allen?" Kevin asked.

"Mrs. Allen huh? Man…" Denise said.

"Hey D, I gotta get something to eat. I'm starving!"

"Ok, Kevin I'll talk to you tomorrow then…I love you. Bye."

Kevin said, "Wait…WHAT!"

Denise laughed. "I said bye." And hung up the phone.

Kevin called her back quickly. She picked up on the first ring. "Hello-ooo" She said.

Kevin laughed. "Nice…you dropped that joint and ran huh?"

Denise laughed.

"You're scared huh?" Asked Kevin.

Denise said, "Duhhh, yeah!"

"It's cool. Can't blame you. Love you too Dee." Kevin said.

"Damn you Kevin! You got me feeling all these feelings and shit!" She said laughing.

"Bye babe. I'll see you tomorrow." Kevin said.

"Bye Kevin." She said as they hung up.

Kevin hung up the phone smiling and turned to see his brother David standing in the doorway just staring at him.

"What man?!" Kevin said to his brother.

"Remember that scene where the Grinch was on top of the mountain and his heart started growing…" David said.

Kevin cut him off. "Man, shut the hell up!" As he started laughing with David.

Kevin walked into the cafeteria the next day and found Bobby, Denise and Abby sitting together at one of the far tables in the back. Denise was intently staring at him as he approached.

"Hey babe." He said as he bent down and kissed her on her cheek.

"Hey Kev. Glad you're here and I won't have to sit here and watch these two eat each other's faces off with their eyes. I think it was a mistake introducing them." She said laughing.

"Oh, for real? Bobby, she got you hooked man?" Kevin said.

"I ain't even gonna lie man…" Bobby said as Abby smiled and blushed. Just then Kevin saw Allison walking their way. He gave Bobby the look to let him know "heads up" and got up from the table and met her half way. "Aye what's up Allison?" He said to her.

"Hey Kevin, is that Bobby over there?" She asked.

Kevin looked at her with a serious face and said, "Over there with his girl, yeah…"

Allison crossed her arms and said, "His GIRL?! She wasn't his girl last week when he was calling me all the time sweating me to go out and shit." Kevin said, "Yeah, that's his new girl. They just hooked up this week. Soooo… you and Bobby used to go out and shit huh?" He asked knowing full well the answer.

"Hell no!" She said quickly.

Kevin smiled and said, "So why you acting mad?"

Allison gave him a look of disgust and said, "I'm not mad. I was just going to say hi. I'll leave him to his little girlfriend if that's what she is…"

And turned and walked away.

Kevin came back to the table and Abby looked at Denise as if she would get mad at Kevin for talking to another female.

"Who was that!" Abby said in a way that relayed, *you're not gonna just disrespect my friend like that in front of us.*

Denise chimed in, "Girl that's Allison, she's on the JV Tennis team. You got practice today?" She said to Kevin.

Kevin looked at Denise surprised at the quick thinking lie she just told and said, "Nah, she was asking me to talk to the coach about getting on the Varsity team and I was saying that it wasn't on me and that she should probably talk to Greg since he's the Number 1 seed on the team. As you can see she got kind of pissed that I couldn't help her."

Bobby just sat quietly looking away and gave himself two short punches in his chest which signaled to Kevin, *Good looking out!*

Abby relaxed and said, "Oh ok."

Kevin looked at Denise wide eyed and said, "Welp, I'ma grab something to eat real quick."

As he started to rise Denise said, "I got you...here."

She reached into her bag and pulled out a Nehi Strawberry soda and a two pack of Krispy Kreme jelly donuts.

Kevin looked at her and smiled.

Denise said, "Partner's, right?"

Kevin's head swung around and he asked, "Seriously?"

Denise smiled and put out her fist. Kevin's face lit up in a smile and he said, "Always!" as he pounded her fist.

Bobby looked over and said, "No shit! Damn good partners too!" and sipped his soda.

Abby looked at Bobby and said, "Awwwwwww... are we gonna be like that?" Bobby smiled and said, "Of course babe." And gave Abby a quick kiss on her lips.

Denise folded her arms and stared at Bobby and Abby and said, "What you think Kevin? They don't look like they're *All in* like us, do they?"

Kevin folded his arms and stared at them and said, "Nah. They're not ready for that."

Abby and Bobby almost in unison said, "What is *All In*?"

Kevin lifted his hand as if to start speaking and Denise grabbed it and said, "No Kevin. Don't do that. Let them have their little thing. On their level. It's kind of cute."

Kevin laughed. "You right, you right. It'd be cruel to tell them about a Cadillac when they're driving a Cavalier."

Abby and Bobby just gave a puzzled look at each other as Kevin and Denise laughed.

Bobby rose from his seat and said, "Yeah ok. Abby I gotta move the car real quick I'll be back."

He looked over at Kevin. "Aye man, smoke one with me real quick."

Kevin rose and left his drink at the table. "Be right back D."

Abby and Denise slid closer together.

"Ok." Denise said.

As soon as they cleared the door and exited to the back-plaza Bobby burst into and excited rant. "MAN, WHAT THE HELL!!! SHORTY GOOD LOOKING OUT GOT DAMN!!!" Bobby laughed.

"I got you Fam." He said as he gave Bobby some dap.

"Shorty Denise is quick with her shit too! You need to keep that one man!" He said.

"I plan to." Kevin said smiling.

"Man, broad ain't never talk to me in school. Now suddenly when she sees me with somebody she got rap for me. Isn't that some shit!" Bobby said.

"That's how folks do man. Don't miss you till you're gone. She's some garbage. Don't even worry about that trick."

Bobby said, "I ain't gonna lie. I felt good seeing her pissed that I was with somebody else."

Kevin said, "You're petty man." And laughed.

"Petty shit! All them miles I drove that broad…call me what you want. That shit felt good!" Bobby said.

"You didn't get kind of mad when you saw Kevin talking to that girl?" Abby asked Denise.

"Nah. I mean it's not like Kevin just got here on Earth, right? He knows other people just like I do. I trust him."

Abby sat quietly and then said, "You didn't strike me as the type that would ever trust any boy when we first met."

Denise smiled and said, "I still don't trust any boy. But I trust Kevin."

Abby tilted her head to the side and gave her puppy look and said, "Awwwwwww…"

Denise looked at her and shook her head, "There you go with that again…jeez."

Abby straightened up. "So, what do you think about Bobby? You think I should trust him? I mean, like you trust Kevin."

Denise looked at Abby and shook her head side to side again and said, "Oh no! That's your decision. That's on you! You won't be coming up to me blaming me if things go wrong."

Abby looked down and said, "It's just that I don't know a lot about…things like this and I figure you do."

Denise laughed and said, "You jive slick like trying to call me a ho?"

Abby sat up waving her hands back and forth and said, "NO! NO! NOOO!!! I'm not saying that! No. Denise?"

Denise laughed and said, "Calm down Abby I'm just playing jeez girl."

Abby put her hand on her chest and breathed deeply. "Wheeww! Don't do that!" Abby's face slowly sank into a sad look.

Denise looked at her with concern as she put her hand on Abby's shoulder. "Come on Abby, you know I was just playing."

Abby pooped up smiling. "I was just playing too! Let's go out again this week!" She said smiling.

Denise moved her hand away, gave her a blank look and said, "Get away from me man..."

Abby laughed and tried to hug Denise and said, "Awwwww... come on best friend! I was just playing!"

Denise kept the blank face. "Nah., You stupid. Get off me..." and hugged Abby back.

"See. You can't stay mad at me!" Abby said as she smiled a ridiculous smile at Denise.

"You try that limit everyday though don't you." Denise said.

Abby continued holding the same smile rocking her head side to side. Denise had to break the stone face and laugh at her. "Soooo stupid!" She said as she laughed.

"What the hell are ya'll doing?" Kevin said as he approached the table. "Just Abby being Abby again" Denise said as she scooted over for Kevin. Bobby looked at Abby. "What you do baby?"

Abby smiled at Bobby and said, "Nothing. Just missed you when you were gone." Bobby's face lit up with a smile.

Kevin looked at his boy and said, "Pitiful…"

Denise chimed in, "See that's that crap I was dealing with before you showed up. Got damn after school special shit right here!"

Kevin looked at Bobby and said, "Ya'll go together now?"

Bobby and Abby said nothing.

Kevin said, "What kind of shit…?

Denise chimed in and said, "Awwwww hell naw! I been dealing with this crap and ya'll don't even go together? What's up with your boy Kevin?"

Kevin looked down at his shoes as if disappointed and said, "Wish I could tell you something D. I thought for sure he was built out of…"

Bobby cut Kevin off before he could finish… "Hey Abby…I was thinking maybe we should go together and be boyfriend and girlfriend. What you think?" Abby's face turned red as she smiled. "Ok…" she said shyly.

Bobby looked at Kevin trying to look hard and not smile at the same time. Kevin then said to Denise, "Remember that thing we were talking about earlier? Yeah. That's what it looks like when a dude's balls finally drop." Denise looked at Bobby and said, "Ohhhhh…that's what you were talking about."

Bobby said to Denise and Kevin, "Hell with ya'll man."

As Abby's hand went up to hold Bobby's. "Leave him alone ya'll" Abby said. Kevin quickly grabbed his side and said, "Bitch!" as he looked at where his hand had grabbed.

Denise said concerned, "What's wrong?" Kevin acted as if he was in pain and said, "I thought something bit me but it was him" as he straightened up and looked at Bobby and said, "Biiiiitch!"

Bobby stood there for a second, smiled and then died laughing.

Denise and Kevin started laughing too.

Abby shook her head and said, "Ya'll are too much!" As she started laughing also.

Abby says, "Hey ya'll trying to go out this weekend somewhere?"

Bobby said, "I gotta work Friday and Saturday evening."

Kevin asked, "What time you gotta be at work?"

"Five" Bobby said.

"Well Saturday my brother is having his birthday party sooo…" said Denise. "Let's hook up Sunday then." Said Kevin.

"Nah. My people ain't gonna let me go out Sunday night before school that's out." Said Denise.

"Ok. How 'bout Sunday morning at around…11am. Cool?" Said Kevin. Denise said, "How about let's not go out and just chill in my basement listening to music or playing pool."

Bobby said, "Bet! That cool Abby?"

"Yeah that's cool for me too" Said Abby.

Kevin looked at Abby and Bobby and said, "Maybe you two should exchange numbers so you can talk on the phone now *(as he grabbed Denise hand and helped her up)* and act like a boyfriend and…what kind of shit?!" as Denise and Kevin walked away.

Denise said, "I know right!?"

Bobby and Abby just sat there. Bobby yelled, "Ya'll wrong for that!

Kevin got home and changed into his beat-up clothes. He decided it was time to check out that Cobra. He figured he'd pull the transmission pan to see if the fluid was burnt, or if there were any clutch pack particles in it. At the least, he was going to change the filter and put in fresh fluid to see if that stopped the slipping. *'Cheapest fix first'* was his mantra.

As Kevin was going down the steps, he saw his dad and mom in the kitchen putting groceries away.

He came into the kitchen and said, "Y'all need some help?"

Kevin's dad smiled up from the bag at him and said, "No Kevin, we've got it."

Kevin thought to himself, *He's been doing a lot of that lately, smiling at me.*

Kevin looked at his mother and said, "We've got a surprise for y'all, so don't have anything planned for this weekend."

Kevin's mother looked at his father and said, "OK, we'll try to keep our schedule clear."

Just like that, Kevin figured out where he got all his sarcasm from.

"Hey brat!" Kevin yelled at his sister who was studying in the next room. She didn't say anything, and just raised her pencil in the air and waved it.

David came into the house with a basketball in his hand, walked into the kitchen, and said, "Hey y'all...where you going?"

Kevin said, "I'm headed to Lucas's garage to pull the trans pan and maybe get that seat out so I can take it to Kelley's to get welded."

David said, "Bet man. Let me grab something to eat, and I'll meet you over there."

"Once you change out of your school clothes," his mother said to David. "Yeah Mom, I'm not going like this," David said.

Kevin laughed.

"Two hours Kevin," his mom said as he was leaving.

Kevin started out the door, then turned back to his dad. "Thanks for helping me with those signs, Dad!"

Kevin's father smiled. "Thanks for fixing the car! A guy was gonna charge me 200 bucks to fix that!"

"Awwwww man!" Kevin remembered one more problem with the car.

"Dad, let me get your keys."

Kevin went outside, popped the hood to the Buick, pulled the air cleaner off, and reconnected the wires to the A/C compressor that the last guy his father took the car to had disconnected, and told him it would cost $700 to repair. Kevin put everything back together, shut the hood, and said aloud, "*A/C fixed*!" He went into the car and set the controls on the dash to Max A/C, then returned the keys to his father.

"You have an hour and 45 minutes now, Kevin," his mom said.

Kevin smiled, kissed his mother on the cheek, and said, "Love you, Mom," As he started for the door.

Kevin's Mom yelled after him. "Two hours, Kevin." He looked back, and she smiled at him.

As Kevin grabbed the door, he heard his father say, "Humph!"

Kevin's mother looked at his father and replied, "I know you're not over there making noises, Uhhhh."

They both laughed.

Kevin got to Mr. Lucas's garage and pulled the door open. There it was! His 1970 Cobra! The one that got away! Kevin was beaming! He walked slowly around the car, taking mental notes. It was some butterscotch yellow color or something. Kevin immediately thought, *Either Daytona Blue or Black.* He looked in the interior and all he could envision is him driving through the park on a warm DC night with the windows down, the sound of that 429's exhaust humming, and Melvin Lindsay's quiet storm cranking out the slow jams with a nice cool summer breeze coming through those windows cooling him down. He even pictured Denise leaning back in the seat in a sundress, sweat droplets on her forehead and chest with her eyes closed, humming to whatever was playing on the radio and smiling that smile. Kevin snapped out of it and laughed at how he'd let himself get carried away. *Come on man, shit. Isn't none of that happening unless you get started on this thing.* He jacked up the side of the car, put stands up under it, slid his socket set under, and then himself.

"Nice." he heard someone say.

Kevin bumped his head under the car and said, "Got-dammit! Come on, David! Make some noise or something!

Kevin started sliding out from under the car. "Don't just sneak up on me, shit!" he said.

Kevin raised himself up on one arm and slowly looked in the direction that the voice came from. The sight before him froze him.

"Bridges!" he said with a fearful tone.

Bridges smiled and said, "Hey Kevin."

Bridges covered his hand with a pocket square, reached down, grabbed Kevin's hand and pulled him to his feet.

"What's up? I do something wrong? Did I, do it? The mission, I mean. Did I, do it?" Kevin asked excitedly.

Bridges looked at the pocket square, then threw it in the trashcan. "Yeah Kevin, you did it. It's done."

Kevin smiled big and just as fast, his smile turned into a look of concern. "Soooo…what happens now. I mean, to me?"

Bridges handed Kevin a lit cigarette. "Well Kevin, you go back."

Kevin stepped back and dropped the cigarette on the floor. "Back to what?! Back to Baltimore?! Hell naw, man, you might as well kill me now! I ain't doing that shit again!" Kevin said as he turned from Bridges, trying to hold back his emotions.

"Calm down Kevin, you changed a life. In doing so, the path of your life changed, too," Bridges replied in a reassuring voice.

"Changed how? And why can't I just live out my life from here?" Kevin asked.

Bridges took a drag from his cigarette. "People, all people, have a predetermined and finite number of years to live. I took you when you were 48. You must return to age 48, to live the rest of your allotted days. The memories of what will happen in this new life are ones you will have when you return. You will have the gift of remembering two lives up until the age of 48. One was bad; one was good. That should help you appreciate the good one that much more."

Kevin stood silently for a second, taking in what was said. "So, I'll have a good life?" Kevin asked.

"You'll see," said Bridges. He put the cigarette out under his foot. "You ready?" Bridges asked as he extended his hand toward Kevin.

"Ho, ho, hold up a minute!" Kevin said as he stepped back from Bridges. "Who was it...that I saved?"

Bridges smiled and turned his head to the side. "Who do you think it was, Kevin?"

Kevin answered assuredly. "It was Abby, wasn't it?"

Bridges laughed. "I knew that's who you'd think it was. No, it wasn't Abby." Kevin gave a perplexed look. "Then, who?" he asked.

"Well Kevin, since you have to know, it was Tiffany. Believe it or not, your brief relationship with her was her wake up, so to speak. She stopped hanging around Cynthia and her group of players, and wound up becoming a good woman, got married and had three kids, one of whom will need to fulfill her destiny as you have. Had you not turned her around, she would have dated a few drug dealers in the 80's; eventually got strung out on crack; lived in shelters; dealt with Child Protective Services, physical abuse, and incarceration; not a pretty picture."

Kevin looked at Bridges in shock. "Tiffany…damn. What about my girl, Mrs. Alexander? Did she finish her mission?"

Bridges laughed out loud, shook his head and wiped a tear from his eye. "Yeah, Kevin, Mrs. Alexander completed her mission quite well I'd say. We talked for some time before I took her back, and she had a very interesting analogy that I've adopted to explain better the task I set forward for new candidates that I send back."

Kevin looked with anticipation and asked, "Which is…?"

Bridges said, "She said she looked upon her mission, herself, as a key, needed to unlock the potential of the future. You all, my candidates, are keys."

Kevin thought about it for a second and said, "Yeah, that pretty much sums it up."

Bridges smiled and said, "I thought so, too."

Kevin smiled and then his look turned grim. "I had so much that I wanted to do differently this time though, …my mother… my father and David. Come on, man, can I stay for a while longer, just so I can say goodbye again, in my way?" Kevin asked as his eyes welled up.

Bridges said, "Kevin, the first thing I want you to do when you get back is to think about all those things that you now want to do. I think you'll be in for a nice surprise to find that you did them. Like I said, you get to keep your memories. They'll come to you over time, gradually. I just can't give you any more time."

Kevin straightened himself out and said, "Cool, cool. OK."

Bridges approached Kevin again, and once again Kevin backed up. "Hold up, hold up! You seem to be able to change history by placing people back into their past, right?" Kevin asked.

Bridges gave Kevin a puzzled look and said, "Yes, that's right…"

Kevin said, "So in doing so, everyone is sent back in time, right?"

Bridges smiled and said, "I already know where this is going, Kevin. The answer is, time is relative. Your measurement of time is not my measurement of time. A second for me could be, if necessary, a hundred years for you and vice versa, if it takes that long to make sure a moment in time was correct. Does that answer your question?"

Kevin said, "That's good info but no, my question is, what's the deal with déjà vu?"

Bridges smiled while nodding his head as he looked down at the ground then back up at him. "Daydreaming," he replied.

Kevin looked at him strangely, "Daydreaming? How's that related to déjà vu?"

Bridges explained. "The memory is erased from people's conscious memory whenever we do a time adjustment. But we've found that when a person is daydreaming, their subconscious holds onto small bits of information. So, when someone says that they feel as if they'd done this or have been at a place before, well, they have, and what they are recalling are the bits of memory that their subconscious had stored. Understand?"

Kevin nodded his head.

Bridges smiled and said, "None of this strikes you as strange anymore I see. You seem to follow this pretty well now, huh?" he asked.

"Makes sense to me," Kevin replied.

There was a moment of silence as Bridges just stared at Kevin as if waiting for something. Then he asked, "So you're not going to ask me why we allowed Hitler to do what he did? Why we allowed slavery?"

Kevin thought a moment and said, "I guess Hitler was a necessary evil to show the world what could happen when we allow the depths of human fears, insecurities, and hatred to go untethered. It's fortunate it occurred in the period it did and not, say, now. With technology as it is today, they may have wiped the whole Jewish population from the face of the Earth. Now slavery, although it pains me to say it, America, without it, would never have become the industrialized powerhouse it is without the labor of slaves. I've got to imagine it was also necessary so the United States would become the dominant military force in the world, to maintain some semblance of order.

Bridges said, "You seem to grasp the fact that sometimes one has to allow violence and evil, at times even participate in it, for the greater good.

Kevin nodded and said, "One more question...will I go to Heaven?"

Bridges smiled at Kevin knowingly and said, "You're stalling, Kevin. David is not going to come through that door if that's what you're hoping. Everything outside of this room has been suspended."

Kevin smiled at Bridges in a way that conveyed to Bridges that he was right. He was stalling in hopes to see David one more time.

Kevin said sheepishly, "Ehhhh, ya got me. I was ju..."

In the time it took Kevin to blink, Bridges had covered the distance between them, took Kevin's hand in his, smiled and said, "Thank you for your service Kevin, I'll see you later."

Once again, his hand glowed with bright light. Once again Kevin passed out.

As Kevin faded away, he faintly heard Bridges whisper, "I may have found a new apprentice in you, Mr. Allen."

Then he too faded away.

Kevin awoke to two smiling faces jumping on his bed shaking him. "Wake up Dad, wake up!" they yelled.

Kevin, Jr., and Danielle, his children, were yelling in his face. He looked up and laughed out loud as he saw Denise, his old school buddy, new girlfriend and apparently, his now wife, coming through the door with a tray of food and a cupcake with a lone lit candle in the middle. On her left hand, he could clearly see a wedding ring.

"Happy Birthday!" they all yelled in unison.

After he ate and opened gifts from his family, Kevin drank his coffee and looked out the window. He could see the tail of a black 1970 Torino in the garage., he thought to himself.

Oh man! I better call Mrs. Alexander to tell her what's going on! as he grabbed the phone and dialed her number.

A soft, younger voice answered. "Alexander residence."

"Hello. May I speak to Mrs. Alexander, please," Kevin asked.

"This is she. With whom am I speaking?" the voice replied.

"I'm sorry. This is Kevin, Kevin from Coolidge. Remember?" he asked. There was a brief silence. "Kevin Allen?"

Kevin got a sinking feeling. "Yes, Kevin Allen. Is anything wrong?" he asked concerned.

"My Aunt...passed away four years ago.... I'm sorry."

Kevin's heart sank. "I'm really sorry to hear that, and my sincere condolences to your family," he said.

The voice came back. "Thank you. My Aunt did leave a note for you that I could send to you if you'd like, or you can come and pick it up."

Kevin looked out the window. "Is it possible that you read it to me?" He asked.

"Hold on," she said as he heard her place the receiver down. She returned shortly and said, "The family has been wondering about this letter for years. Were you a teacher or her student?"

Kevin answered, "Her student."

She replied, "Oh ok."

Kevin heard an envelope opening and paper unfolding before she continued.

> *Dear Kevin,*
>
> *If you are reading this, it can only mean that I have gone on to Glory. I hope you are doing well. As it turns out, you were the mission that I was to complete. I followed your life as much as I could, asking about how you were doing when I'd run into your classmates here and there. As you suggested, I let Abby come and live with me after she graduated, and she turned out to be a real blessing for me, a great help around the house back then. She made me so proud when she told me she wanted to follow in my footsteps and became a teacher. I felt as if I were watching the daughter I never had when she walked across that stage to receive her degree! It was a great idea getting her and your friend Bobby together, too. She can't stop talking about him! They tell me your sign business is doing great, and that Denise is doing great as a family therapist.*

You two were made for each other. Enjoy your second chance Kevin, as did I, and continue to be an inspiration to everyone you encounter. You never know how your small acts of kindness can dramatically affect someone's life!

A fellow Key,
Gwendolyn Alexander

Kevin listened with tears welling up in his eyes. "How did she…" he started to ask.

"Aunty died peacefully in her sleep," the tearful voice chimed in.

"Your aunt was very special. If there is anything I can do for the family, please let me know," Kevin said sorrowfully.

"Thank you, Mr. Allen. Goodbye."

"Goodbye," Kevin said as he slowly hung up the receiver.

Kevin reflected on what he'd heard. *I was her mission…my 6th grade teacher Mr. Woods was probably the plan A that Bridges referred to that was supposed to turn me around. Then Mrs. Alexander…plan B…plan B…,* he thought to himself, looking out the window and trying to piece everything together. *How many other keys did I walk amongst that I didn't know were there?* His mind thought back on every pleasant person he'd ever meet. *How many who have not completed their missions do I walk amongst now?*

'She died peacefully in her sleep…' That, for some reason, brought some relief to Kevin. *We all have a finite number of*

days, he thought as he shook his head. *I should try and enjoy mine…*

His peripheral vision caught movement to his left. Bridges was waving his hat back and forth in the air to get Kevin's attention.

He smiled big up at the window at Kevin and held his thumb in the air as if to ask "Ok?"

Kevin smiled and put his thumb in the air to signal back to Bridges, "Ok."

Bridges held a small box in the air and then placed it in Kevin's mailbox, tipped his hat, started off down the street, and then faded away.

Kevin sashed his robe tightly around his waist and walked outside toward the Cobra. He noticed a sun-bleached hat with a Mustang emblem on the rear shelf in the back window. He opened the door and removed it. On the inside brim, it read: David Allen.

He remembered David giving him the hat shortly before he died and him saying, 'Keep this in the Cobra for me so you'll always remember me'.

Who could ever forget David. He thought to himself.

Kevin put the hat on his head and walked toward the end of the driveway to get the newspaper and check the mailbox.

Just then, a DC Police car slowed and the window rolled down. The officer yelled to him, "Kevin…Kevin Allen…?"

Kevin yelled back, "Yeah...."

The driver parked his car and out came a huge police officer, smiling big. "What's up, man! Long time no see, bro!" he said as he 'dapped' Kevin and hugged him.

Kevin smiled back and said, "You look familiar as hell man, but I can't place the face..."

The cop took his cap off and said, "Henry, man! Henry Chandler from Coolidge!"

Kevin laughed a laugh of relief. "Man, when you first jumped out of that car, I got to thinking, what the hell did I do?"

The officer laughed. "You did a lot is what you did, man! I know you remember that big fight me and Reds got into on the side of Coolidge that day."

Kevin recalled it. "Yeah I do! You were swinging your ass off. You lost, but you kept swinging!"

They both laughed. "Yeah, that's what I remember most about it is you kept yelling, KEEP SWINGING!" Henry said.

Kevin laughed. "Well, you definitely did. It was ugly, but you did!"

The cop said, "Yeah, but it was enough to get them dudes to stop messing with me! Since that day, all I wanted to do was be a cop so I could help people out the way you helped me out. I've been on the police force 25 years now, and I ain't leaving until I can't do it anymore!"

Kevin shook his hand. "That's what's up, Henry!"

The cop started back toward his car. "Kevin man, if there's anything I can ever do for you, let me know bro!"

Kevin yelled back, "You already did, man! Good seeing you!"

He watched from his driveway as the car pulled away.

Damn..., he thought to himself in amazement. *Every single interaction with someone could be the one that changes someone's life...forever.*

He reached into the mailbox and in it was a nicely wrapped square box that read:

> To: Kevin Allen
> From: Bridges

Taped to the box was a card.

Kevin opened the card.

> *To one of my most animated Keys. The work is never over.*
> *Enjoy and make the most of your days Kevin.*
>
> *-Bridges*

Kevin opened the box to find a platinum skeleton key mounted on a chain inside. He smiled as he placed it around his neck. Just then it occurred to him that he had seen many with necklaces just like this throughout his life.

He walked back into the house through the side door, where he found Denise clearing the dishes.

"Don't forget we're going out to celebrate with Abby and Bobby tonight," Denise said over her shoulder. "Did you hear me, Kevin?" she turned around to see Kevin just standing there smiling at her. Denise was about 40 pounds heavier with gray streaks in her hair that fell curly at her shoulders. She had small wrinkles around her eyes and mouth, but that same smile. *Beautiful,* he thought to himself.

Kevin started singing:

> *"Mother nature must have made you,*
> *You've got a smile that could rise the sun..."*

Denise slumped her shoulders and smiled. "You know that's my song right there. Don't start nothing you can't finish Kev!"

Kevin walked to her, hugged her deeply, kissed her on her neck, and whispered in her ear, "Thanks awesome girl."

Denise turned around and kissed him on the lips and hugged him tightly. "Happy birthday awesome man, love you too."

She looked at his necklace and said, "That's nice, where'd you get this?"

Kevin smiled and said, "Dee, when we're real old and gray, I mean REAL old, remind me to tell you a story about Bridges."

The End

CPSIA information can be obtained
at www.ICGtesting.com
Printed in the USA
BVHW031442030121
596829BV00006B/463